Spellbinding Stories

by

Dolores Allen

ISBN: 1-4140-6045-9 (e-book)
ISBN: 1-4140-7977-X (Paperback)

Library of Congress Control Number: 2004090490

This book is printed on acid free paper.

Printed in the United States of America
Bloomington, IN

1st Books - rev. 02/25/04

Acknowledgments

I am grateful to everyone who believed in me.
*****

I wish to give a special thanks to Catheryn Gertz, my professor at the University of Windsor for her encouragement. She made me believe that my stories should be published.
*****

Thank you to my friends and loyal readers in Millville.
*****

Thanks to Lesley and Ann at 1st Books Publishing.
*****

To my dear friends, Lu and Bill Vos, Thank you.
*****

A special thank you to my friends and relatives in Windsor, Ontario who have read my stories and kept me believing that I had a special gift for story telling, and to Dan for encouraging me to enroll in the University classes.
*****

A special thanks you to my Aunt Evelyn and all my relatives in Hainesville, New Brunswick.
*****

A very special thank you to my husband, George, for believing in me, and helping me throughout the entire process. With his help I am happy to say, my dreams have come true.

*****

A word of gratitude in advance to all of my readers.
Dolores Allen

Words of Praise For the Author

These stories touch and warm your heart, drawing you in- making you eager to read more...Kae Dubel

Dolores' stories are compassionate and intensely moving. I love every one of them...Michelle Enright

Dolores Allen is a wonderful storyteller. Once we started reading her stories, it was hard to put them down. We found her stories to be most enjoyable...Bill and Lu Vos

Dolores Allen is able to capture the reader's interest and keep them wanting more. Her short stories are compelling, intriguing and ...truly spellbinding... Richard and Anna St.Antoine

Dolores has written stories filled with nostalgia, and real people. Courage and faith are in the forefront. They are filled with emotion and they are all so different...Owlyn Aitken

Spellbinding stories make you want more. The author has written from the heart... Keep them coming Dolores...Gwen Little

Dolores gives a true picture when she writes. She has stories for all ages and all people. Can't wait for more...Zelma Williams

Dolores' stories are wonderful, and so full of inspiration as well as down to earth. They are told so vividly that one may think that he/she is there. Her stories are heartfelt and you find that once you begin you cannot put them down till you have finished the story... I send warmest wishes to the author and cannot wait to read her book...Juanita and Brian Nicholson

Dolores' Spellbinding stories truly touch the heart. James Allen PHD

Memorials

Dolores writes in detail about the events before and after the horrific fire on Friday 13th, 1946. This story is a must to read. Part one captivates the heart and Part two is just as compelling. The tragic loss of a father, brother and son brought me to tears. Her courage inspired me...GPPP.

This was the day I learned what empathy meant by actually feeling grandmother's pain. Knowing all about sympathy was one thing, but empathy was different. I knew what it was like to lose someone you loved deeply. She lost her son, my father, when he was 36 years of age in a house fire. It was on a cold, rainy, foggy day like this day that my mother shouted. "Jump out the window. The house is on fire! You must run to grams now!"

That dreadful day washed over me like it was yesterday. As I raced forward on my bike, I began reliving that horrific day once again. I cried out, "will this nightmare never go away and leave me in peace?" The memory of my words made me shiver. "This is not really happening. I will go back to sleep and when I awake it will be just a dream." It was not a nightmare it was real. It was so real I could taste the smoke and feel the heat from the fire. Hearing my mother's voice once again screaming, "get outside, hurry!" My father was downstairs engulfed in flames. The kerosene can that he was using to start the fire exploded. He became so disoriented he did not know how to find the door. When he finally did get out, his clothing was in flames and his body was badly burned. My mother kept screaming for my brother, John and I, to jump. The fear of jumping was almost as bad as the fire. I went back to bed and covered my head with blankets, still believing it was a dream. Suddenly, realizing that my brother was not in the room with me, and that I was alone, a thought came to my mind that perhaps it would be safe to go down the stairs and creep out the front door to safety. Upon reaching the top of the stairs, in a crouched position, a sudden giant orange flame reached the top of the staircase. It felt like long hot arms were coming to get me. Knowing that this was impossible, I crawled to the bedroom window, and looking down, I saw my mother. She was shouting in a raspy voice, "jump I will catch you!" I shouted back, "I'm afraid, I can't jump." I noticed little pieces of clothing burning on the ground. My father was rolling in the snow to put out the fire. Smoke was overtaking me, and I felt sick. The flames were getting hotter. They lit up the house in an orange flare and the sky seemed to be the same vibrant color. Father stood up and saw me by the upstairs bedroom window looking down. It was then that he realized I was still in the house. He quickly walked toward the house, and stood bravely under the window saying. "Sara jump! I will catch you." I jumped and he caught me. I was safe. How can this be happening? My father was so strong and brave and now he stood in front of his family with skin peeling from his naked body. This is a scene that has been played and replayed in my memory like an old horror movie for many years.

My brother and I stood shivering in the snow wearing our nightclothes. The cold and fog was nothing to what we were feeling inside for my father. Mother was telling us to run to grams. We began running in our bare feet in the snow as fast as we could to grandmothers. An angry dog was barking in the distance. Grandmother stood with a look of disbelief when she finally opened the door.

Father gave in to the pain and suffering that afternoon at a quarter of three. It was December 1946, on Friday the 13th. Christmas lost its spirit, for my brother and I, for many years.

Table of Contents

Save the Best for Last   1

Lady in Red   11

A Miracle for Patrick   19

Love Letters   29

A New Season   37

Tropical Dream   43

A Dark Side   47

Rosie and her Sister   57

Pole Hill   61

Merry Christmas   67

Nora's Tragic Mistake   73

A New Family   81

My Friend Robbie   87

Saving Martha   91

Humor versus Poverty   97

The Snow Tunnel   101

Mystery under the Elm   109

The Gift   117

God's Special Treasure   123

The Reunion   131

A Dying Prayer   137

Homeward Bound   143

Hidden Treasures   147

Save the Best for LastPart 2   151

Save the Best for Last

By Dolores Allen

Driving up the hill that overlooked the small community made me sad. So many changes had occurred during my absence. It had been so green and plush by the ledge where I sat many times as a young girl. Now it was covered with moss, broken branches and twigs. It seemed so desolate. "Did anybody else ever come to this place that I held so dear?" I asked myself. I felt such a sense of place, and could think clearly here. The tragedies of the past would begin to make some sense.

Sitting down on the moss was like sitting on a soft cushion. The musty smell of dampness triggered a feeling of sadness, and yet there was a sweetness that came along with it. Gazing over the village below and trying to recall the joy and happiness I felt as a young girl was an easy task. Sitting here for hours and daydreaming about far away places became a wonderful adventure.

Everything seemed so right with the world in the early years, no worries, cares, disappointments or betrayals. The word, "betrayal" seemed to leap out at me. Yet, as I recall, it was the best of times. I hungered for the good old days, for my parents, my brother, my son, my grandparents, but they were gone from me forever. It was times like this, remembering my grandmother's words, "the best is yet to come, dear," gave me hope. She had another saying, "save the best for last." Never knowing quite what she meant by that, it still made some sense. I wondered what great things were ahead for me, or was it just false promises? I had many dreams. They were kept alive for awhile. My dream of becoming a writer was my special desire. Wanting this so badly, I could feel and taste it.

Longing for the day that I could leave this little community and travel to far away places became the main goal. I wanted to be successful, and make grandmother proud. I did attain a certain amount of success in business, but it did not seem to be fulfilling. I never stopped dreaming my dreams, I just put them on the shelf, I suppose. Material things were not satisfying. Travel did not seem to put out the fire. Never knowing what I was looking for kept happiness just round the corner.

Sitting here in the silence, gazing aimlessly, there appeared in the sunlight a tiny piece of broken glass with a blue tinge. It was embedded in the moss. Pulling it out and staring at it as if in a hypnotic state it brought on horrific sadness, and in an agonizing moment all the past came rushing in consuming my thoughts. Running my finger over my hand I felt the rough scar on my right palm just below the wrist. The scar and indentation had not faded any more than the memory of that awful day when I delivered the bad news to my grandmother that her sister Betty had suddenly passed away.

Memories were returning vividly sitting here thinking of my grandmother, and recalling the long ride to her house that day. My heart was pounding again, as it had that awful day so long ago. The mist was in the air and tears were blinding my vision as the bike lunged forward. Suddenly the front wheel slid to the side, and left me reeling to the gravel. A piercing pain from a piece of blue glass that was hanging from my hand. It plunged deep into the soft tissue just below the wrist. Gravel was embedded deeply into both bony knees.

My stomach began to feel sick. Licking the salty tears that ran down my cheeks, the bike carried me onward. My hands were tightly gripped on the handlebars. The tears were not from the injury, but for a much deeper pain that would soon be shared by someone I loved. "Must stop crying, don't want to upset gram anymore than necessary. Must try to be calm and brave by the time I reach her house." The words were spouted out loud.

The weather was cold. Rain was freezing on the road, and the fog was so thick you could cut it with a knife. I could feel it in my bones. With teeth chattering and blood dripping from one hand and both knees, I peddled on. So many thoughts raced through my mind on that trip to grandmothers. "Why does it always have to rain when bad things happen? I hate the fog and rain. I want sunshine. When will the sun ever shine? How long will I have to watch my grandmother cry and grieve this time? I wish things could be the way they were yesterday." I muttered tearfully. "How can she go through this again?"

This was the day I learned what empathy meant by actually feeling grandmother's pain. Knowing all about sympathy was one thing, but empathy was different. I knew what it was like to lose someone you loved deeply. She lost her son, my father, when he was 36 years of age in a house fire. It was on a cold, rainy, foggy day like this day that my mother shouted. "Jump out the window. The house is on fire! You must run to grams now!"

2

That dreadful day washed over me like it was yesterday. As I raced forward on my bike, I began reliving that horrific day once again. I cried out, "will this nightmare never go away and leave me in peace?" The memory of my words made me shiver. "This is not really happening. I will go back to sleep and when I awake it will be just a dream." It was not a nightmare it was real. It was so real I could taste the smoke and feel the heat from the fire. Hearing my mother's voice once again screaming, "get outside, hurry!" My father was downstairs engulfed in flames. The kerosene can that he was using to start the fire exploded. He became so disoriented he did not know how to find the door. When he finally did get out, his clothing was in flames and his body was badly burned. My mother kept screaming for my brother, John and I, to jump. The fear of jumping was almost as bad as the fire. I went back to bed and covered my head with blankets, still believing it was a dream. Suddenly, realizing that my brother was not in the room with me, and that I was alone, a thought came to my mind that perhaps it would be safe to go down the stairs and creep out the front door to safety. Upon reaching the top of the stairs, in a crouched position, a sudden giant orange flame reached the top of the staircase. It felt like long hot arms were coming to get me. Knowing that this was impossible, I crawled to the bedroom window, and looking down, I saw my mother. She was shouting in a raspy voice, "jump I will catch you!" I shouted back, "I'm afraid, I can't jump." I noticed little pieces of clothing burning on the ground. My father was rolling in the snow to put out the fire. Smoke was overtaking me, and I felt sick. The flames were getting hotter. They lit up the house in an orange flare and the sky seemed to be the same vibrant color. Father stood up and saw me by the upstairs bedroom window looking down. It was then that he realized I was still in the house. He quickly walked toward the house, and stood bravely under the window saying. "Sara jump! I will catch you." I jumped and he caught me. I was safe. How can this be happening? My father was so strong and brave and now he stood in front of his family with skin peeling from his naked body. This is a scene that has been played and replayed in my memory like an old horror movie for many years.

My brother and I stood shivering in the snow wearing our nightclothes. The cold and fog was nothing to what we were feeling inside for my father. Mother was telling us to run to grams. We began running in our bare feet in the snow as fast as we could to grandmothers. An angry dog was barking in the distance. Grandmother stood with a look of disbelief when she finally opened the door.

Father gave in to the pain and suffering that afternoon at a quarter of three. It was December 1946, on Friday the 13th. Christmas lost its spirit, for my brother and I, for many years.

My grandmother sat silently by my father's still body until he was buried on a cold windy winter day. I saw such pain in her face. Understanding her grief was almost more than my brother and I could bear. It matched our own. We thought that we would not be able to live without our father. "Who will take care of us?" We thought we would surely starve. My brother and I knew our lives would never be the same. We wondered if we would ever be able to feel joy again.

Grandmother had tremendous strength that she passed down to her son and I believe some of it came to me. My father and grandmother shared the same compassionate blue eyes, and a kindness that always made me know that I was loved. They won many battles over the years. My grandmother survived cancer when she was young. She survived widowhood, and raised 6 children. My father was persecuted for being born out of wedlock. To us he was a hero. He was the most handsome man on the earth, or so I thought. One of his sayings was, "a man is as good as his word, if his word is no good then he is no good." My father never stayed angry, and he always put his family first. "He was as good as his handshake." He believed in working hard, telling the truth, and never owing money to anyone. He passed his values down to my brother and I. He was a great storyteller. He could make you laugh or scare you to death.

I was nine and a half years old at the time of my father's accident and the loss was almost unbearable. I did survive, but my brother never learned to cope. He suffered great sadness and anger, then one day at age 28, he decided to end it all, with that he placed a gun in his mouth, and closed it forever. It left no marks on his face. My life took a horrific nose-dive after that tragedy. He was my special friend and grandmother's favorite grandson. Just one more struggle for an already sad grandmother.

Sitting here brings back so many memories, some wonderful, but this day mostly sad times. Some say we are not given more than we can handle. The bad things are just God's way of testing us. Sometimes I did feel, "why me?" But I knew that it was just self-pity.

My mind drifted back to the task at hand, as I was getting closer to gram's house. I kept saying, "be strong and don't cry." My mother always said, "only babies cry." No matter how hard I tried the flood of tears came fast and hard. Gram saw me approaching the house and welcomed me with outstretched arms. Encircling her plump body with my arms, I gave her the news holding her as tight as possible. With my face buried in her breast, we wept our hearts out. She cradled and comforted me, then she began to wash my knees and remove the broken glass. In her time of grief she thought of me first. The feeling of love for my grandmother that day has remained with me always. Lying cradled in her arms for some time, we cried for her sister and my father.

All of a sudden, grandmother stood up straight with composure and dignity, saying, "I must go up the road now, will you come with me?" We walked side by side holding hands up the bumpy gravel road. The mist lay heavy on our cheeks. She breathed heavily, as we took those quick steps, to the sadness that lay before us. As we approached the farmhouse where her sister lay, she lifted her snowy white apron to her cheeks, and with a rapid motion wiped away the tears. My gram smiled down at me. By the way she squeezed my hand, I knew she was telling me, "everything was all right."

Now looking below, and remembering all the love, I wonder why I was so eager to leave this place that offered so much. Guess it was because I had a restless spirit, and wanted more out of life than this community had to offer. Some say I was an adventurer, perhaps they were right. I think I was running away from the sadness and loss of December 13, 1946, the day my childhood ended. Thinking that my leaving would be a happy experience, and life would be so much better, was just a delusion. The dream of becoming a successful writer, also became just that, a dream and nothing more.

Life has many twists and turns. I did eventually leave the community. The dreams of becoming a writer faded. It died a quick death like so many other things.

I married at a young age, but that part of my life is something I have spent many years trying to forget. It did have a positive note as it gave me three sons. My youngest boy loved the hill. He spent many summers with me here. He had a kind spirit like my father, and a sweetness that allowed everyone to love him. He was my special friend. I sometimes felt that he was trying to replace my brother. When I divorced his father, he helped me in many ways. When I returned to school, he would dictate letters, late into the night, for my shorthand class. This enabled me to speed up my shorthand. Having a part time job, school, homework, and other tasks, I found it difficult to keep up the housework. He would help in every way possible. He was proud to show me how he had cleaned the apartment while I was at work. I would praise him. He smiled with joy at my pleasure. He understood that going on my own was the best for all. We were safe now. It was a glorious feeling.

I would write to my grandmother and tell her my problems, but many times, when things were going well, I would let too much time elapse between letters. She never stopped writing to me. She always wrote such encouraging words. She would say things such as, "you know dear, you can always come home." She never complained about her life, she only counted her blessings. She had so little. I always thought that, if I ever earned enough money, I would buy nice things to make her life better. Realizing it now, she never wanted fancy things or money, she only wanted a short letter or a visit. Sitting here and thinking, "I wish I could do it all over again" was painful. I never told her that I loved her. She knew I did. The only hugs I got in my early years were from her and my father. They both loved me unconditionally.

I began to spend most of my time working, thinking of little else. It became my passion. "So why am I sitting here on this hilltop remembering only the sadness in my life?"

Holding the piece of broken glass was bringing thoughts of despair. The glass represented a broken spirit and that spirit was mine. The heaviness in my heart was dreadful.

All at once there was a sweet presence. Sensing my son was nearby, I turned and looked around, knowing that would be impossible, but the feeling was very strong. "Is that you son?" I said out loud, but of course there was no reply. The sharp realization that he would never be here on this hill with me again made me sense the same horror that I felt the day he took his last journey. That was the day it felt as though someone had turned off all the lights.

I began to think about the last trip I made to the London hospital to see him. It was a lonely trip. I had suitcase in hand and a determination to stay in that city until I was absolutely sure he was better. He was taking far too long to recover. I prayed all the way there. The two-hour drive gave me plenty of time to talk to God, and beg him to make my son well. In another hospital they had told me he would be going home in a couple of days. When there was no sign of a recovery I insisted he be sent to a University Hospital, feeling that he would have a much better chance of a complete recovery. I knew that he would be safer there and get the treatment he needed, after all he was only 37 years old. He had to get well. As I prayed, and began thinking about my own mother losing a son at 28 years of age and my grandmother losing my father at age 36, I suddenly felt a dreadful fear. It sent chills over my entire body. I started praying louder and begging God in an angry voice. "Please don't take my son, haven't you taken enough from me already? My son is too young and too many people need him."

As I drove in the hospital parking lot that morning there was a feeling of urgency. I ran to his room. His first words were, "Mom feel my legs and see if they feel like grans." He was referring to my mother who had lost her battle with cancer two years earlier. She had remained in our home until her passing. He remembered her legs becoming ice cold the day she passed away. I felt his legs, they were cold and stiff. I ran to the desk and asked the nurse in an angry voice, "is my son dying?" With that she said, " what do you mean?" I then told her about his legs. She rushed to his room and instantly paged the Doctor. When the Doctor approached the desk he looked grave. He asked me to remain in London for a few days. He gave me the dreaded news that my son had a fast growing cancer, and that they could do nothing for him. He said it would only be a few days. It was not to be. My son left me the following morning, at 7:20 A.M. to join my mother, father, brother and grandparents. We held hands all night. He kept repeating, "Love you Mom." We exchanged words of love and encouragement. I continue to write to my son on special occasions. I know now that God knew best and took him from his suffering. He was only ill for six weeks. I am grateful for that.

My thoughts are interrupted, knowing that it is time to go down the hill and start packing for my journey back to the real world. I hate leaving this place even though it does bring back much sadness. I still feel a sense of place here.

There is no escape from my memories. This is a place of reliving sad times and happy times. This was a time of remembering sadder times.

"I promised myself one quick stop at the cemetery to say goodbye to my mother, father and grandparents. I know they are not there, but it is a feeling of being connected. I am thinking how wonderful it would be if my son could be with me. He went with me so many times in the past. He loved my mother and he cherished my father's memory.

Mother always said she wanted her ashes put with my father when her time came. I was pleased that she felt that way even though we lived many miles away. She was 28 years old when she became a widow. I am not sure that she ever recovered from the death of my father. She never talked about him, and rarely spoke about my brother. She may have discussed her grief with others, but not with me. I often wonder if she went to her own hill. If so, she never let me know. It was on a Monday evening that she made a peaceful exit to be with my father and brother. I had told her earlier in the day to feel free to go and join them. She was aware that I was capable of handling it. Being anxious to join them she left us that evening with her arms raised to the ceiling. There was a look of peace that I had never seen on my mother's face before. Seeing such sweetness, I said, "mother you are beautiful, you look like a china doll." I am absolutely sure she is with her husband, son, and grandson. This gives me some pleasure.

As I am preparing to leave, a car approaches. I wonder if someone else enjoys this spot. It looked so deserted. I assumed that no one had been there since my visit a year ago. Walking to the car, a man approaches. I thought he looked vaguely familiar, but I did not recognize him. He introduced himself with the kindest voice, and then the memory came alive. With a smile, I said, "a stranger from the past." "Not a stranger for long I hope," he replied. With that we sat down and began to talk about the past. We shared so many things. I asked him if he came here often, he replied, " every time I am home on holiday, it is my favorite spot." We talked for hours reliving so many past experiences. We were hungry to catch up on the past. I told him that I had always visited the hill on each visit. We shared our successes and failures. I told him that this was where I came to daydream as a young girl. He talked about his past. We shared a lifetime in one afternoon on our hilltop. Before we knew it, darkness fell. We began laughing and acting like children again. We were so engulfed in learning everything about one another that we did not notice or care how late it was. Learning that we both shared many sad times made it easy to confide in one another. We laughed and shed a tear or two. I kept thinking about my grandmother's words, "save the best for last," and "the best is yet to come." We exchanged addresses and phone numbers. Driving down the hill, my heart felt light knowing that the best was yet to come. I also knew in my soul that this was just the beginning of the best. After saying goodbye to this wonderful person from the past, I felt like a young girl again. He became that same sweet young boy. "Yes gram, I did, save the best for last. The lights are back on."

To be continued.

Lady in Red

By Dolores Allen

The black water was churning, first to the left, then to the right in an unfriendly manner. Foghorns were blowing in the distance. Fog was rolling in fast. Oliver could hardly stand the churning in his stomach. He was going home, but to what, he wondered. The old ferryboat was worn and rusty. The guardrails creaked each time the boat swayed back and forth. The ropes were black from age and they looked frayed as though they might come apart from any hard tug. It started out to be, what he thought, would be a cold and tedious ride.

"Maybe if I go inside for a moment the churning will cease," he thought. One step into the archway, and just left of the stairs that led to the lower lounge he saw, what he thought was a delusion. Standing, and looking out over the rail into the moonlight, was the most beautiful girl he had ever seen. He thought his imagination was running wild. A piece of work he thought. That's what his navy buddies would have called her. They had a saying for everything. That was their favorite expression for a pretty girl. She was truly a work of art. This red headed girl turned and looked directly into Oliver's eyes. He knew that she was secretly flirting with him. Pretending he did not notice he turned and left the room.

Oliver was a young sailor. Tall, dark, and handsome was the accurate way to describe him. His mother told him that he was so handsome in his uniform that he should be in the movies. Without question he was an outstanding young man. "You turned many a young girl's head," his grandmother jokingly told him. He had dimples in his cheeks when he smiled and a strong jaw. His good looks did not take away from his masculinity.

Under the dimly lit lamp, just outside the cabins, Oliver stood and gazed at the moon. He listened to the many sounds of the ocean. The roar of the engine in the old ferry chugging along was a mournful sound. Several times, it seemed to hit and miss. The moon shining on the whitecaps looked like shimmering sequins all gold and silver. Many times the water became almost invisible when the fog intensified.

Oliver's thoughts went back to the girl he had just left inside. He wondered if she was real. Her dress was fire red and she donned accessories to match. Her hair was almost the same shade as her clothes. Her legs were long and her stockings had long black seams up the back. He noticed everything about her as she walked away. Her tiny waist was accented by her above average bosom. She looked like an angel. "Oh, stop thinking these things," he said to himself. "You have a girlfriend at home. But, will she be waiting?" Oliver was not sure of anything anymore. The last letter he received from his girlfriend was a bit cold and now he was unsure of her commitment.

The chill was in the air, and it was time for Oliver to go to his cabin. "It will be a long night on the ferry and I should get some rest," he thought. He looked down at the polished buttons on his uniform and shiny shoes. Somehow it gave him such a sense of pride knowing he was a Navy man. He would joke with his brother who was an Army man saying; "the Army is fine, but there in nothing like the Navy." He did look striking in his pressed uniform. The trousers hung with razor sharp edges down the front and the bars on his collar shone under the light. Standing there admiring himself was rewarding. Now it was time to move on and get some rest. Heading for the archway again his heart jumped. There before him was the lady in red. She was slowly moving toward him with a look in her eye that he knew only too well. "My name is Lucille. What is your name?" She asked in a husky voice. She sounded something like Lauren Bacall, he thought. "I'm Oliver, why are you going to St. John?" He asked. She answered again in her soft, but husky voice. "I am meeting relatives in St. John. They will drive me to New York. I live in New York City. Are you on leave or are you going home to stay?" Before he could answer, she took his hand and pulled him to the railing. They stood holding hands and looking into the swirling dark waters below. Somehow the water and the ferry did not seem so cold and unkind as it did earlier. They stood for a long time in silence. Suddenly they turned toward each other and they knew they wanted to be close. She was warm and soft. He felt the need to hold her tenderly in his arms. The evening air was damp and cool but they did not notice. The only thing they felt was the warmth from each other. They wanted to learn all they could about one another in this one night. Oliver held her and caressed her. The feelings that he felt for Lucille were something he did not understand. He had just met her so, how could he feel such tenderness and maybe even love. "No, it couldn't be love they had just met," he thought.

Sometime in the middle of the night he walked with her to her cabin and kissed her good night. He wondered, "How am I going to wait until morning to see her?" He slowly strolled to his cabin. He closed his eyes and could almost feel and see Lucille in his arms. He knew that vision would remain with him forever. He had never seen such beauty. Lucille was not just physically lovely, she was sensual. When she walked it was seductive and alluring. When she looked at Oliver he knew it was a look that said she wanted to be with him. He lay on his bunk with closed eyes trying to relive every moment of the evening he shared with her. "I must never forget one single moment. I will keep this evening in my memory for the rest of my life," he thought.

The morning was bright and sunny. The foghorns did not sound so mournful as they had the previous night. It would not be long before they reached their destination. He would have to say good-bye to Lucille. When she approached him she was holding a piece of paper. "This is my phone number and my address. If you ever come to New York, please call me. I do not want this to be the end. Promise me you will keep in touch." Oliver began to tell her about his girlfriend back home, but the loud noises from the boats that were leaving the dock blocked out the words. She never heard. When it was time to say good-bye they held each other and kissed long lingering kisses. Oliver had never been kissed like that before. Lucille clung tightly to him. Her legs were shaking and tears were beginning to well up in her eyes. She began to cry softly. Seeing the tears, he bent over and kissed them away. He held her close and promised her that he would see her again.

The drive home from St. John was a long one. He was not eager to see his girlfriend now that he had found such love and peace in this strange girl's arms. His thoughts were completely on his lady in red.

When he arrived at the station his mother was waiting at the gate. She informed him that Sally would come over to the house shortly. Oliver's answer was "who?" "You know, your girlfriend," his mother answered laughingly. Once he was settled in the house a knock came on the door, and Sally entered. She was pleased to see Oliver. Sally was a good girl and would make a good wife for him someday. He also knew that she would be an excellent mother to his children should they have any.

He could not get Lucille out of his mind. "What if I never forgot her? What kind of a life will it be for Sally and I?" He asked himself. He knew that many people had wonderful lives without the kind of attraction that he and Lucille had for one another.

The time passed quickly and now it was time to go back. Somehow he did not mind leaving home and returning to his ship. The thought that he might be docked in New York harbor one day was not hard to take either.

Several months passed and the thoughts of New York harbor were out, however a leave was in the forefront. He quickly made up his mind to go visit a relative in New York. He knew it was just an excuse to see Lucille. The first night he arrived at his uncle's home he explained that he needed to see someone. His uncle understood and told him to call at once. Oliver let the phone ring several times, but no one answered. He felt such disappointment. His uncle told him he should have written or called a few days before he was to arrive to assure that she would be there. "Oh well," Oliver said, "I will try one more time and, if she is not home, it is okay." He put his suitcase in his room and hung up a few clothes then he returned downstairs to where his uncle was sitting. He began to tell his uncle the story about how he met this beautiful girl and about his girlfriend back home. He confessed that he felt total confusion about his feelings. Uncle Jim grabbed the phone and handed it to him. "Call and keep calling until you find her," he said. Oliver dialed the number slowly and on the second ring Lucille in her husky voice said, "Hello." Oliver's voice began to quiver. He was shaking all over. "Lucille, this is Oliver. Remember on the ferry?" Lucille screamed in the phone. "Where are you, are you in New York?" "Yes!" was the reply. "I would like to see you tonight if possible, please give me some directions," he shouted. His voice was reaching a high pitch from the excitement of seeing her again. After several minutes of chitchat he was on his way to the streetcar. His uncle asked if he was sure he knew his way. He said that he did. "I'm a big boy," he yelled at his uncle, as he ran out the door.

The ride on the streetcar seemed to go on and on. He knew that he was going to come to his station soon. Each station was numbered, but he could not read the number until he was nearly there. The closer to the stop the more excitement he felt. This was his first ride on a streetcar. He spent most of his days on ships or docked in harbors.

A large lady wearing a wide brimmed bright yellow hat was seated in front of him. She reached up and pulled a cord and the car came to a screeching halt. The smell of iron as the wheels slid on the rails smoked and gave off a distasteful smell. "Was this his station he thought?" Looking out the side window he saw Lucille standing by a post wearing the same red dress. She was even more beautiful than he had remembered. He already remembered her scent. His mind could conjure up her sweet smell at any given moment. Before he knew it, they were standing close in each other's arms and laughing for what looked like no reason at all. They were enjoying the moment. "Let this never end, Lucille," he was whispering in her ear. Once they regained some composure they started walking slowly down the street toward her house.

Her parent's home was huge and painted white, with many windows. It was situated close to the sidewalk. The lawn was well manicured. Attached to the front of the house was a long verandah with scalloped trim around the top. Along the side of the steps sat fancy flowerpots with blossoms of all colors, showing off their exquisite beauty, for all the neighbors to enjoy. Lucille motioned him to sit on a swing that was placed in front of two large windows. Oliver was sitting in a position where he could view the entire living room. By a huge stone fireplace was a baby grand piano. It was jet black and had a sheen as bright as the buttons and bars on his uniform. He began to have a sinking feeling. Instantly a sadness came over him. He knew that he did not belong in this rich girl's life. He could never give her this kind of a luxury. He did spend the night there at her parent's house, but with a heavy heart he left the following morning. The night was a night he would remember forever. It would bring a smile to his face, but also a tug at his heart. Missing Lucille never ended. She remained in a secret place in his heart. Red became his favorite color. He visualized the stockings with the black seams going up the back of those long pretty legs for years. The good-bye was a sad one. He tried to make it brief. When he walked down the steps toward the sidewalk he did not look back. He feared that Lucille might be crying and he did not want to see her sadness.

The war was nearly over, and Oliver was not looking forward to returning home. He had begun to enjoy the excitement and adventure of the Navy. He liked how he looked in his uniform and the structure the Navy provided.

Letters kept coming from Sally. He knew that she expected to get married as soon as he was discharged from the Navy. He knew that she was a great girl and came from a good family. Being a down-to-earth, home spun gal he knew that she would make a good companion for him.

The fall came quickly and Oliver was on his way home for good this time. Sally was waiting at the station with his parents. She did look pretty, wearing a new flowered dress, and new shoes with black seamed stockings just like Lucille's. Her hair was piled high on her head. Oliver stared at her, thinking how glamorous she looked. That evening when they were out walking in the cool fall air, he asked her to be his wife and they set the date. They were married just before Christmas.

Life moved along quickly, and Oliver became very successful in the ministry. He even became elected as mayor of a prosperous city. He achieved every goal he set for himself, and his life with Sally was very good. He raised wonderful children. He adored his grandchildren. Life was almost perfect, but Lucille never left his mind completely.

His loyalty and love for Sally grew over the years and they were truly blessed with a great life. He believed that by serving God it made everything complete. Having strong convictions he also believed that God gave man two hands, one to provide for himself and his family. The other hand was to help others. He was a giver. He raised his family to be unselfish and to walk the spiritual path.

After many years of family life, Oliver found himself alone. The house felt empty and sad as he sat by the window missing Sally. He wondered how long it would take to get used to living alone. He had many friends, and the church was a great support to him, nevertheless he felt an emptiness.

One evening in the late fall he was sitting by the fireside reading when the phone rang. He was so startled that he nearly leaped out of his chair. "Hello," the voice said in a raspy voice, "is this Oliver? Were you on a ferry many years ago going from Digby, Nova Scotia to St. John, New Brunswick? Do you have an uncle in New York?" Oliver's heart began racing. He thought he must be dreaming. He whispered into the phone, "Lucille, is that you?" He could not keep back the emotion and before he knew it they had filled in all the blanks of the past years. He told her why he had never returned. He said, "you looked so rich. I knew that I could never give you all the material things that you were used to having. I felt it was for the best if I didn't see you again." He shared his successes with her. He told her of his sad times. They tried to recapture some of the lost years in one short phone call. Before they hung up they promised that they would write and send pictures.

When a week went by Oliver found a large envelope in his mailbox. He was so excited that he could hardly wait to tear it open. He knew it must be from Lucille and that there would be pictures inside. There she was, dressed in a red dress with white hair and a smile that no man could resist. She was as beautiful as ever. Oliver phoned her immediately and thanked her for the pictures. She had received his, as well. She told him that he was still as handsome today as he was then. He told her that she was still the most beautiful girl in the world. With this they had a few giggles. Oliver reminded her that they were in their sunset years. She reminded him that it is never too late to love and be happy.

They are planning a meeting in the spring. A ferry ride is on the agenda. It is doubtful if they will say good-bye this time.

A Miracle for Patrick

By Dolores Allen

Eric and Patrick sat quietly on the old broken bench in front of the railway tracks. Everyone said the rows of steel were coming out soon, but so far no one was working on their removal. The old station house still stood with broken windows. Nearly all the shingles had vanished. Perhaps the high winds did the destruction, who knows. The old days of waiting for the train with the red flag waving in the gentle breezes were gone. "How long has it been since the tracks were used?" Eric asked his friend Pat. He sat looking at the ground and with a slow motion he shrugged not knowing the answer to the question. He felt sad every time he came here remembering the bitter disappointment in his youth. A long time ago Patrick or, Pat as his friends called him, sat on the same bench, waiting for the train to stop. The chugging sound and the screeching of the iron on iron was a warning that someone or something was getting off the train.

Remembering back to that bright sunny day in July, and the joy, he felt that late afternoon, was a feeling of true elation. He was about to see his mother for the first in time in five years. He stood there remembering her long blond hair and her little turned up nose that moved when she smiled. "How could he remember so many details when he had been so young?" He wondered. The excitement rose with every passing moment. He visualized his mother dressed in a bright flowered dress, donning high heels. "Yes, she would be carrying a huge bag. That would mean she was staying for a long

19

time. Maybe she would never leave this time," His imagination was running wild.

Looking up the tracks, beyond the curve in the rails, he could see black smoke in the distance. Suddenly, he jumped at the sound of the loud toot and whistle, just north of the station. Pacing back and forth he felt his emotions rise to the point of tears.

The train was coming around the curve at full speed. "Why is it not slowing down?" He wondered. Before he knew it there was a loud whistle and the train had pushed on past the station. Pat stood there in total shock. "Why had the train not stopped?" He whimpered. His mother was on that train. She would hold him in her arms and kiss his tears away. He was eager to carry her suitcase and smell her sweet perfume. This is what he had waited for since his fifth birthday. Every night, for the past few years, he lay in bed dreaming of her return. The joy he would feel at their reunion. He could see her running to him and smiling. The embrace would go on forever. "That's what Mothers are supposed to do," he thought.

Eric was staring at Pat wondering where his mind had drifted. "Hey buddy! Where have you been the last ten minutes?" He asked, half joking. Pat looked up and down the tracks, and with a sudden gesture he waved Eric to follow him. "No! Eric retorted I am not going anywhere until you tell me what you were thinking about. You were so deep in thought and your face was covered with sadness." Pat walked back and slumped down on the bench. He lowered his face in his hands and began to weep. "Eric I just had a flashback of a time when I was ten years old, and it was a very sad time indeed." Eric prodded once again, wanting to know what had happened to bring back such sad memories. "Perhaps someday I will tell you, but not right now." Pat whispered. "Okay then," Eric replied.

Walking up the long hilly road was an ordeal for even the strongest young men. The ruts were deep and on both sides of the road lay huge rocks. The gravel was hard and sharp under their feet. Both were wondering why they took this walk so often. It was a long way, but they did enjoy the quiet and solace. They felt that just being in such a deserted place was pleasant. There was a feeling of being in tune with the universe.

Pat and Eric had been friends since grade school. Eric realized one day that he knew very little about Pat. He knew he was a kind spirit, but a bit distrusting when it came to girls. He was always on guard. Eric on the other hand was completely opposite. He trusted everyone. He was a tall boy with blond hair and deep blue eyes. A quick smile was one of his assets and everyone felt good around him. Pat loved being with Eric as it gave him a feeling of belonging. When Eric went places he took Pat with him. Otherwise, Pat would have been a loner. He was well on his way when he met Eric at a park one day. Eric took an instant liking to Pat. They became good friends quickly, even though they attended different schools. It was unusual for Pat to trust anyone so completely, but he trusted Eric right from the beginning. So why had he not shared any of his past? He was not sure himself why he kept his sad times a secret. He had no reason to be ashamed.

The two young men trudged slowly up the third long steep hill when both began to laugh, "why do we do this?" They asked of one another. Eric replied in a laughing voice, "I guess we just like punishment."

Pat was a handsome young man with dark hair and a tanned completion. His eyes were almost black with a look of mystery, and a glint of sadness. Even when he smiled his eyes, unlike Eric's, were dark and dusky. "What was behind these obscure eyes? What secrets did they hold?" Eric wondered.

When they reached the top of the last hill Pat sat down on a huge boulder and motioned for Eric to join him. Pat began speaking very slowing while staring at the ground. His friend lowered his eyes in the same fashion as though he knew something serious was about to unfold. Pat began in a whisper by saying. "Eric, you always ask me each time we are sitting by the old station house why I look so sad. Well, I will tell you, One day a long time ago I waited for that train. I was full of excitement waiting for my mother to arrive. I had not seen her in five years. When the train went screaming by, I thought my heart would break. I waited such a long time to see her. She was not there and never did come back. As the entire story unfolded, Pat kept his eyes on the gravel between his feet. Eric listened intently to every word. He felt the same emotion, as his friend. Pat started back at the beginning. He told Eric how one night when he was tucked in bed at his grandmother's house, his mother Jean sat down by his bedside and began to talk in a soft voice. She said, "Pat I am going away for awhile. You will remain with your grandmother. I know it will be hard at first, but it will be better in the end. You are different than other children. You did not have a father to help you. I know how difficult it has been. You are brave and strong. I have never talked about your father or explained what happened. I think the time has arrived for you to know. About one month before you were born, your father left for a holiday in Europe. That was the last time we were together. I saw him off at the train station and I have never laid eyes on him since. We were left destitute, that is the reason we came to live with your grandmother. I could not manage on my own. Your grandmother has taken very good care of you. That has given me an opportunity to continue on with school. I will leave in the morning for New York. As you know Pat, I have been studying acting. I hope one day to have a chance to play on Broadway. I cannot get anything going here. I must be close to the action, where I can go and audition. This is the only hope I have. I will come and get you when I earn enough money and can take care of you. Until then you will have to remain here. Please do not be angry with me. I have a good chance right now to be in an off Broadway play. I must try. Please wish me luck. I promise I will return soon."

Pat turned to Eric and smiled. "So you see that is why I was so disappointed that day at the station when the train did not stop. I was sad and angry at the same time. Walking home that day I thought that I hated her. I cursed her under my breath. I would repeat over and over again, "I hate you." When my grandmother died last year it was impossible to let my mother know because I didn't know where she was or if she was even alive. I read the cast of every Broadway show to see if perhaps she might have a starring role, or even have a bit part, but to no avail. I even thought she might have changed her name, or worse yet be dead." Eric moved over and put his arm around his pal and hugged him hard. "Thank you for sharing this with me. I had no idea that you had suffered such losses. What about your father, did he ever try to find you? Where is he in Europe?" Eric questioned. Pat told him the only thing that his grandmother had told him was that his father's name was Dino Valente and he was from Italy. She told Pat that was where he got his dark completion, dark hair and eyes. She said he was much like his father, but Pat had never even seen a picture of him. He wondered if his father was as insecure as he was? He wondered who he was really like, his mother or his father? Both had abandoned him.

Eric on the other hand was very secure in his youth. That carried on into his adulthood, unlike his friend. His parents were still together and he had a wonderful childhood. He was always told how smart he was. He grew up with great self-esteem. He was outgoing like his folks, taking an active role in the community, heading up many organizations for fund raising. Everything he did, as an adult seemed to be for the good of others. It came naturally. He inherited all the good qualities of his parents.

As the years passed, Eric became more and more successful in his business. He began traveling to many countries, and had little time for his friend Pat. When he moved his factory to another part of the country, they seldom saw one another.

Pat tried to keep in touch with his good friend by phoning, or sending the occasional card, but one day he lost interest. He felt that Eric had outgrown him. Their lives had gone in different directions. Perhaps they had nothing in common anymore. Pat went to college and learned the trade as a millwright. Eric ran a tool and mold company. Both of them were in the same line of work.

Eric was on a plane for Italy when he suddenly remembered that Pat's father was Italian. He sat in his seat, with his head in his hands, trying to remember his father's name. He drew a blank. He decided that it would be hopeless to try to find this man. "He is probably dead." He said to himself. Lifting his head he took a magazine from the pocket on the seat in front of him. There was a name that sounded familiar. The Italian airline that he was flying had a picture of the president on the inside cover. Under the photo he read, "Dino Valente." "That's the same name," Eric said out loud in an excited voice. "Could it be the same Dino Valente?" He wondered. With that he began feeling lonely for his old friend. Guilt began creeping in. Thinking to himself, "why did I let so many years gone by without keeping in touch? How could I have let such a good friendship go?" It left him feeling sad. The man in the seat next to him began talking at that moment, sending the thoughts of Pat adrift as quickly as they came.

Years went by slowly for Pat. He remained in the old farmhouse that he had shared with his grandmother until her death. He loved the old house with its drafty windows, creaky floors and musty smelling basement. The wind whistling around the corner of the barn was an eerie sound. It was a reminder of where he belonged. Every winter morning, when he cranked up the old wood furnace, he felt such a sense of place. The smell of the firewood burning, and the heat rising from the floor grate, gave him a safe feeling. It all spelled home. One morning as he sat outside on a tree stump that had been there since he was a young boy enjoying the quiet, his thoughts drifted back to the good times that he had shared with Eric. He sat looking across the road. Snow banks, that had once been pure and white, were now dirty and black. The fog was drifting in scattered patches across the field. The river was covered with shades of white and gray with funnels of fog lifting up, as if they had some spiritual power moving them to and fro. The mist was cool in the air. There were two birds perched and pecking at the ice. They began to appear and disappear as the fog made a shield while it moved and swirled around them. The eerie feeling that Pat was feeling was something he had experienced before. He felt uneasy. "Something is going to happen," he said, "and I am not sure it is something good." Suddenly, he put the feelings aside, and began walking to the house.

Many weeks came and went. Soon it was spring and everything was in full bloom. The dirty snow was gone and the birds were singing their cheerful tunes. Pat was getting ready to plant his garden. Looking out to the road he noticed that the flag on his mailbox was lifted. He meandered to the newly painted mailbox. Inside was a thick letter from Europe. "Who could that be?" He thought. Inside was a long letter from Eric. He began the letter by asking Pat to forgive him for being so neglectful and not working to keep their friendship. Pat wondered why he was asking forgiveness. He knew that he was as much to blame as Eric. He continued on and the more he read the more excited he became. Eric told him of his work and wondered if Pat would be interested in moving to the West Coast and working with him, since they were in the same line. At the very bottom of the page Eric wrote… P.S. "Can you meet me at the old train station on July 13th at 4:00 PM?" He went on to say that they would talk about it then. Pat ran into the house and immediately wrote his answer. "Of course, he would be interested."

The garden was producing more vegetables this year than any other year. The flowers were knee high and bright reaching for the sunlight. Many colors filled the landscape and Pat became misty eyed when he thought of how happy his grandmother would be if she could see the beauty of the flower garden. Another thing crossed his mind. "Would Gram be upset if he moved and sold or rented the homestead?" "No," he thought, "she would be happy for him to have a new life." He was sad and lonely a great deal of the time since her death.

It was getting close to Eric's arrival and Pat was beginning to get very excited. "It will be great to see my old friend again." He whispered to himself. He wondered if Eric had ever married, or if he had a family? So many questions, but no answers yet. "Why is Eric so interested in me now?" He murmured. Oh well, soon he would see him in person and then he would fill in the gaps. So many years had passed and he knew that there must have been many changes.

Pat finished his lunch and proceeded to clean up the kitchen before he started the long walk to the station house. Suddenly he changed his mind and went back and got his jeep. He had not been there in years, and was unsure of the roads. "Better to ride than walk," he thought. When he finally arrived he noticed the red flag hanging on the side of the station. He laughed thinking, "Eric is playing some kind of joke." The bench was still there, but more worn down and leaning a bit to one side. "Where is Eric?" He was asking himself. Being certain that he would be along any minute he sat waiting and remembering the day long ago when the train sped by leaving only dust and a young boy with a broken heart. He could still smell the heat and the dust and feel the wind from the hurried up train. His throat began to choke up and his eyes became blurry just remembering. With shaking hands he wiped the tears away and visualized his mother in a pretty flowered dress. He imagined the sweet smell of her perfume. Her embrace was real. He had never let go of the warm feeling he got when she kissed his cheek and breathed on his face. Her throaty voice was a sound he recalled many nights before he went to sleep. He would pretend that she was still there singing him a lullaby.

In the distance he heard a sound, but he knew there were no trains. The train had stopped many years ago. "Where could the sound be coming from?" He asked himself. The rattle was loud and the steel on steel left no doubt that there was something on the tracks. He stood up and ran to the middle of the rails. What he saw coming around the bend was a small rail handcar with a motor. He did not remember the cars having motors. He guessed they must have. It looked like a car that was used years ago to tote workers to and from jobs repairing tracks. As the car approached, he thought he saw three people on board. There stood Eric being his old happy self. He was waving frantically, laughing so loud that he could be heard above the motor and clanging of the old rickety tracks. "Who was sitting on the seat beside Eric, was the big question?" He thought. Smoke was starting to drift from the wheels as the brakes slowed the machine. When it stopped Pat could see a man with silver hair and dark skin and a lady wearing a pretty flowered dress. His heart started to beat faster and faster. "Who are they? Could they be? No, he said to himself. They must be friends of Eric." He ran and gave Eric a hug. Eric held him for a long time and when he stopped he looked at his old friend with such seriousness that Pat wondered what had happened. "Patrick," Eric began, "you told me a story a long time ago. I hope you will

25

not be angry with me, but I recalled what you said on a trip to Europe. I decided then to try and find your father. I was successful and he was open to meeting you. He has many regrets. This is your father, Dino Valente. I also decided to look for your mother. She has been very ill for many years, but she was willing to come with me even though it created some hardship. She did not return, that day when you were at the station, because she was hospitalized. There have been many bouts of illness for the past several years. She believed that you would be better off with her mother because she could not give you the care you needed. She was in a mental care facility for ten years. Since that time she has lived in a home with some supervision and is on medication that must be taken daily or she will fall back into the same confused disorder. I have brought her to see you. I know the train is several years late, but today it did stop, and it stopped for you, my friend. May I present your Mother and Father. Your father has a very good reason for not returning as well. When he could return it was too late. All ready too much time had gone by, therefore he just stayed away. He did marry a few years later and had one son who died in a plane crash three years ago. His wife died at age 42 from a rare virus, which she contacted while they were on a safari in Africa several years ago. Dino blamed himself. He has been very lonely. He is very pleased to have found you. His family is gone and now he wants to create a close relationship with you, even though he is late. You can be very proud of him. He became very successful in Italy. He is the president of a large Italian airline. You can be proud of your mother as well. She managed to get some success on Broadway in the early years. They both hope that you will forgive them. Your father cannot speak the language very well, but he will understand a smile and a hug." Pat turned and starred at the two people sitting in the car and without hesitation he ran to them with smiles and hugs that seemed to last forever. No words were needed. When his mother came down from the car he noticed she had two large suitcases. She smelled like a flower garden and her hair was still blond and shiny. Her face was as sweet as he had remembered. He felt like he was looking into a mirror when he looked into his father's eyes. He knew this was his father. Waiting all these years and wondering who he was and why he had left him was a question that needed answers. "Your father wants you to go to Italy with him when he returns to meet your cousins, aunts, and uncles. Will you do that before you decide on working with me?" Eric asked. "I am so confused right now I don't know what to say or do," Pat shouted in an ecstatic voice.

Later that evening they all sat in the farmhouse looking at pictures and exchanging stories of the past. Pat learned that Dino had many problems with the Canadian immigration. He had been deported for being in Canada illegally. He was unable to return. He fought the government for years. After a while he gave up. He looked at his son with sadness and said in broken English. "I thought it would be best if I let you and your mother carry on with your life. I was unsure if things would ever get straightened out. I thought that both of you could make a good life without me. I am so sorry, I was wrong." He did disclose that he had sent money to Pat's grandmother for child support. He asked her not reveal it to anyone. Pat remembered seeing some large bank deposits when he was going through his grandmother's things after her death. He wondered at the time how she obtained so much money at one time. He quickly forgot about it until now.

The evening turned into a week and it was time for Pat's mother to return to the facility. Dino woke up early that morning. When they prepared to leave, he asked Jean and Pat to return to Italy with him. He said that he knew of special doctors in Europe that might be able to help. Eric made one quick phone call and in a few minutes it was settled. All four headed for Europe together.

Dino, Jean and Patrick, as he is now called, have settled in sunny southern Palermo, Italy. They have enjoyed the climate and culture for a couple of years now. Jean still has problems, but she is living with Dino and basking in the sun, and enjoying the salty waters of the Mediterranean. Patrick has found a sweet Italian girl. They will marry in the early spring of next year. Eric was disappointed that his friend did not join him, but happy that he has a great position with his father's airline. Eric and Patrick are better friends than ever. They see each other every time Eric has a business trip to Italy. They have promised they will meet in the Canary Islands every winter for a long vacation together.

Love Letters

By Dolores Allen

The ice had just melted yet it was still a cold night when Nancy climbed over the remaining snow banks to her Aunt Sally's house. Her aunt had been ailing the past few days. Nancy was very weary, but the desire to visit her aunt was more compelling than her weariness. She thought about the joy that her aunt had given her when she was a little girl. She played with her endlessly. The swing that hung on the limb of the old maple tree was still there. The old rope had now turned black and weathered, but the rotted out strands still dangle from the branch. Nancy smiled as she walked by the tree remembering how many hours her Aunt Sally had pushed her higher and higher. "Push me higher Aunt Sally!" Nancy would scream with laughter as the swing swayed back and forth. What memories she had of those early years.

She wondered. "How long Sally would be with her?" She hoped she would live for many years. She was feeling some better these last few months and even appeared happier.

She stepped on the porch only to find the snow had drifted high. She could not get the door open. She pushed and poked at the snow and finally the door began to open. Entering the main hall she shouted, "Aunt Sally where are you?" There was no response from the kitchen or the bedroom. "Aunt Sally! Its Nancy, where are you?" She looked in the bedroom and as she approached the bathroom she saw her aunt laying face down on the

29

floor. In her arms she was clasping a stack of letters tied up with a red ribbon. Nancy took the letters and put them in her handbag and ran to the phone to call for help. She felt that it might be already too late.

The paramedics arrived quickly. They rushed down the hall and into the bathroom. In a quick motion they had Aunt Sally on her way to the hospital. Nancy drove behind the ambulance, her body trembling and fearing the worst. Her fears were well founded. As she approached the desk, the nurse called her aside and told her that the doctor wished to speak with her. She was ushered into a tiny room with many strange odors that made her feel dizzy and nauseated. She was asked to wait, and told that the doctor would be in shortly.

A tall stern looking man with white hair and a sad face entered the room. He said, "I'm Dr. Preston. I am the physician that tended to your aunt when she arrived here a few minutes ago. Are you her closest relative?" With that, Nancy replied that she was. Dr. Preston began to speak in a very soft tone. "Your aunt had a massive heart attack. As hard as I tried, I was unable to save her." He said how sorry he was and asked for the name of the funeral home. Nancy sat there stunned, not believing that this was really happening. Nancy knew her aunt had been ill, but she never believed that it was that serious. She sat quietly feeling the tremors shake her entire body. She was unable to control them. She felt completely alone. Aunt Sally was her mother's younger sister. She was more like Sally's big sister than an aunt. She was Nancy's only remaining relative. The loneliness swept over her. She felt as though a giant hand was reaching out and snatching everything from her. She wept uncontrollable sobs. The nurse asked if she would like the Doctor to bring her a sedative. Nancy did not answer. She just stood up quickly, walked down the corridor and out the door. She did not know where she was going or what to do next.

Lonely and bewildered she woke up early the next morning with a start. She remembered the letters in her aunt's hand as she lay on the bathroom floor. She felt a sense of intrusion as she began opening the letters, but she felt she must. She wondered if there would be some answers to what Sally's last wishes might be. She opened a short letter. It was from an old friend Aunt Sally had not seen for many years. She wondered why her aunt had not mentioned this person in many years. She began to read. It was a warm letter telling her Aunt how happy he was to have been reunited with her again after so many years. He said, "I must admit I have rarely though of you over the many years, but since seeing you again I think of little else. I am not sure why, and I will not question it. I will only enjoy the moments that you are in my thoughts." He asked her to respond and tell him all the things that had taken place in her life over the last several years. He seemed so hungry to learn all about her. The letter was very touching, and now Nancy could not wait to read the second. Aunt Sally had the letters in order as they were written. This letter was full of life's experiences. He was most willing to share many personal things from his past and present. He thanked Sally for the letter she wrote in response to his first letter. He sent regrets regarding her many losses and the sadness in her life. He was so sympathetic to all her woes. He, too, shared all the sad times in his past. It was plain by the second letter that they had connected in a big way. She still could not understand why Aunt Sally had rarely mentioned this special person.

Sally had never married and remained with her mother until her death. There was a closeness between the mother and daughter that was revered by all who knew them. Folks would say, "Sally is so kind to her mother," It did seem as thought they were closer than most. Aunt Sally treated Nancy more like a daughter than a niece. She was a special person in a spiritual way.

Nancy was orphaned when she was five years old. Her mother and father were killed in an automobile accident. She depended on Sally and her grandmother for everything. They took her to live with them the day of the accident and she never left until she went away to college at age eighteen. Nancy graduated and pursued a teaching career. She went to work at a school in her hometown. She taught mentally challenged children and loved the rewards she received watching the progress of these special youngsters. She kept her life private visiting her aunt three times a week after her grandmother died. She knew how lonely Aunt Sally had become after grandmother's death.

Nancy was a bright young woman. Her grandmother said, "she had a heart of gold just like Sally." She had a softness for people that were underprivileged and lonely. She knew a bit about loneliness, but all in all she did feel very fortunate that she was blessed with a loving grandmother and a wonderful caring aunt.

Nancy was a tall slim girl with bright red hair. She resembled her Aunt Sally. Some said she looked enough like her to be her daughter. When she smiled her eyes wrinkled up in the corners and it gave her a mischievous look. She did not want for anything money could buy. Sally was not rich but all her savings were invested wisely. Without a doubt she did this with the future of Nancy in mind. Now Sally was gone, as well as her parents and grandmother. Nancy had lost the last of her family. The pain was enormous. She felt a dark shadow had fallen over her and a heavy cloud was crushing her chest. She was consumed with grief. "How could she ever get over this?" She whispered to herself.

Now looking at the third letter Nancy realized that her aunt and this friend were sharing many private and personal thoughts. The friendship was building rapidly. The third letter talked about a telephone conversation that they were trying to arrange. It was to happen in two weeks. When Nancy was near the end of the letter she realized one more thing, they were planning a meeting in the near future. Who was this person? How could they have so much in common in such a short time? These letters did not sound like anything Aunt Sally would respond to, but she must have. Eagerly she opened another letter, here he mentioned an evening at the beach long ago. This gentleman's name was no longer initials as in the first letters. His name was Joe and he lived in a city many miles away. Nancy had never even heard of the city. She had no idea where it was. With this she took out an atlas, found it on a map and rapidly returned to the letters. Joe talked about a night at the beach and how he had barely remembered it. But, now the memory had taken over his thoughts completely. He wondered if she had remembered. He reiterated that he spent many hours recalling that night. He went on to tell her how many emotions she had awakened in him. Joe confessed that he had not felt any emotion for a very long time due to much unhappiness in the past. The tenderness and emotions began to reappear when he read her letters. "She must have sent him beautiful letters for him to respond in such a fashion." Nancy thought. He talked about the poverty they endured as children and how they grew up. The memories kept coming back. They were reliving them one by one. Nancy was reading in a frenzy. She was dying to find out if they did go through with the meeting. She thought about it, and she remembered her aunt did go away for a week a few months ago. I wonder, she thought, "could she have gone to meet Joe? No! She would have told me what is going on?" Now Nancy could barely wait to get to the next letter. The next one spoke lovingly to Aunt Sally. The first paragraph said, "I must confess I go to sleep many nights with you on my mind and I wake up many mornings thinking of you." Nancy thought, "this Joe sounds like a treasure." On and on she read. The letters became more and more tender and loving.

Nancy finally stopped reading. She needed a break plus she was beginning to feel like such an intruder. Her eyes were feeling weary from the tears she had shed and the intense reading. She started to see her aunt in a different light.

Aunt Sally was beautiful when she was young, but she was not young anymore. She just looked like any other woman of her age. What did this man find so attractive about her to conger up these intense feelings he spoke about in his letters? He was surely smitten by her. This was very obvious. "Another thing," Nancy asked herself, "how did he get so many emotions from just writing letters? Could this be possible that two people could fall in love by just writing letters?" She had heard of these things happening, but never really believed it was true. Yet, every indication was, from what she read so far, Joe loved her aunt. Nancy felt all weepy again and decided she had to know if they did have an opportunity to meet. She continued to read more letters.

The next letter she opened, she noticed it was signed, "affectionately, Joe." The next letter said, "you sent your love to me. I did not know if it was just a friendship love or if you meant it in a special way. I will find out. I will take it, that you did mean it. I am so happy you did say it, because I love you too. I have wanted to tell you, but I was afraid it would not be received in the right spirit. Please meet me at the place we talked about on the phone. I must see you now. I cannot wait for another year. I want to see you as soon as possible. Please arrange it." Nancy hurried up with the next letter and was astonished to read that her aunt had sent him word immediately that she would meet him at once. "Of course!" Nancy thought, that was her hurried up trip. I thought she looked rather radiant, and she laughed at everything, after her return. That was something that had alluded her ever since her mother had died. Nancy began opening the letters with shaking hands. She was shocked that her aunt had kept this secret from her. It did not take long to find out why. Joe was married and did not want to make their plans known until he was divorced and free to marry. Joe always asked about Nancy in his letters. Sally must have told him about raising her after her parents were killed. Joe seemed to know everything about the family.

Nancy wondered if Joe had known her mother and father. She also asked herself, "why did Joe and Sally lose touch with each other for so many years?" So many questions that perhaps the letters could answer if she kept reading. Joe told Sally in one of his letters that his parents had moved away and gave him very little warning. He stated that he was heartbroken when it came time to leave. He wanted to see Sally and tell her, but he could not bring himself to say good-bye. He said the night on the beach was one of the happiest times of his life. He had never stopped loving her. Nancy began to cry as she recalled the sadness in her aunt's eyes over the many years. The loneliness was unbearable for Sally and now Nancy knew why, but her Aunt chose to stay alone. She never did marry, she just tended to her mother. She spent many hours helping Nancy with homework and being like a real mom to her. The bond between the two grew and they became almost inseparable. Nancy wondered if she would be like Aunt Sally and remain single. She longed for someone to love her like Joe loved her Aunt.

Nancy tore open another letter and there it was… just what she wanted to know. Yes! They did have this planned meeting. The long letter gave great insight into what had transpired during that week. The words that described their time together were the most explicit account of what they felt for one another. They were sure of their love. He thanked Sally for the love she had shown him. He said words like, " wanting to spend a lifetime together even at this late stage of their life." It was so tender and loving. The future they planned that week was spelled out in every detail. He talked about the kindness that she gave him and how she changed his life. He said he would never love another. He made many promises to her. He said he really believed they were soul mates. They would love one another forever. It was like coming full circle. He gave every detail of their reunion. It was as if he felt he must write about it so he would never forget. He talked in detail about future plans, He was most eager for them to marry and start their life together. It was to be a challenge as they had many obstacles to bear. He told her that he would never lose her no matter what he had to do. He said he had waited a lifetime and nothing was going to take this love away. The determination in his letters left no guessing where his heart lay, and what he intended to do. Nancy wept as she read every detail of this romance. It was beginning to look like a romantic novel. It seemed as though it was meant to be. As she read his words over and over in the letters. "It is God's plan," she whispered, "Yes, it was in God's plan, but why did Sally have to die before her dream of happiness could be realized? Why God, did you take this dream from my dear sweet Aunt?" Nancy lay her face down in her aunt's pillow. She could smell the delicate scent of Sally's powder. She cried softly, and as the morning broke she could feel the chill in the air. She walked to the window and looked out over the landscape. The dew lay heavily on the grass, where the snow had melted. She wondered how she would face the days ahead. She could not believe she had spent an entire day, and nearly all of the night reading these letters. There were so many letters, cards and reminders of their love.

She went to the kitchen to make tea and decided she would read the remaining letters a little later. Her curiosity got the better of her. She hurried back to the letters. When she thought she had read them all, she began packing them away. Suddenly she noticed a very recent letter that had gone unnoticed. There was a large heart placed at the bottom of the page. Nancy was eager to read this last one, as it was the most recent. She gasped as she read the lines. Joe wrote that his divorce was final and he would arrive at Sally's house on Dec. 24th in the morning. "Oh my goodness!" Nancy screamed, "that's today!" Joe was arriving today and with that she read on. "Sally, I will arrive early and we can start making plans for our wedding. We have wasted enough time already." He went on to say, "we must tell Nancy at once that she is our daughter and not your niece. I only wish you had told me about her years ago. I want to make up to her and to you for all the lost years as quickly as possible."

Suddenly Nancy was full of excitement and the sadness began to subside. She knew she would not be alone. She would have Joe with her. "It was in God's plan." She thought. "I don't even know this man who is my father, but I love him from his letters." She answered her own question. "You can learn to love through letters."

A New Season

By Dolores Allen

"The leaves have left us, another time, another season, it won't be long and it will be Christmas." Megan uttered under her breath as they drove down the desolate highway. "Wonder why no one travels this road any more? The new highway seems to be the route everyone takes." Her husband Max, of 14 year's, barely answers. Megan no longer wonders why he is so silent or even cares.

Max was only seventeen when he quit school and took a job in a factory. Being a middle child in a family of three, he seldom was heard, or that was his perception. He was smaller than his older brother Bob, who was six feet with an athletic build, and a broad smile that made the girls hope it was just for them. It seemed as though all female classmates had a crush on him. Max, on the other hand was slight in build and artistic. He spent his time reading books and learning as much as he could on gardening and building. His smiling blue eyes were just one of his charming attributes. He never lacked for attention in school, but at home it was a different story.

Max wondered why his father, John, rarely spent any time in the house with his family. When he did, he rarely spoke to his wife or the children. It was his mother, Sara, who was the chatty one. She always had time to talk with the boys and their friends. John spoke occasionally, but it did seem like an effort to be friendly.

John was a somber man most of his adult life. People thought that he was an anti-social, uncaring person. His wife gave up, early in their marriage, expecting any kind of communication with her husband.

Sara was extremely proud of her children. The boys were growing into handsome men. Their daughter, Annie, was a beautiful young girl. Max had a wholesomeness about him with such a kind spirit. It appeared that he had inherited his mother's good personality and sweet smile. That was about to change. John had a great family, so why was he angry with his son most of the time, was a question that needed answers. His children could not understand the reason for his mean ways.

As time passed, Max and his father became more and more estranged. By the time he was in his mid teens there was total silence. Max was not sure which was worse, being ignored or the nastiness.

One cold stormy night when Max was about nineteen he returned home to find his clothes on the front porch. His mother greeted him in tears, telling him that his father had gone into a rage and was responsible for this unkind act. In haste, Max gathered everything that was scattered about, and left the house telling his mother that he would never return. He said, " this has nothing to do with you, but I cannot tolerate father's rudeness and uncaring ways." After begging and pleading with Max to remain at home, his mother finally gave up. She kissed her son good-bye, saying that perhaps it was best for all concerned.

After finding an apartment close to his work, Max began writing in his spare time. He found a peace in writing and a healing was taking place. The anger he had felt for his father was disappearing and he began visiting his mother again. John still ignored him, and many times refused to speak to the boy at all. Upon telling his parents that he would marry a young lady he had gone to school with, John sneered, and showed signs that he did not believe it. Sara was angry at her husband's behavior, but she was happy for her son. She hugged him and wished him well.

Max and his mother were swept up in the wedding plans. She was especially excited over the closeness it had created between her and her son. She began helping with the arrangements.

When Sara met Megan she liked her instantly. The feelings were returned. As the wedding day drew close, the young bride to be began to notice that Max was taking on his father's personality. He was beginning to stay silent a great deal of the time. Sara noticed it as well. She began to question Megan. "Have you noticed the changes in Max?" "Oh yes," replied Megan, "but I thought that he was just stressed out with all the wedding plans." Megan took on a look of deep concern and asked her mother-in-law to be if she thought she should go through with the wedding plans. Sara reassured her in a calm voice. "Everything will be fine Megan, once the wedding is over and the pressure if lifted, besides it is too late to stop the plans now."

Megan began praying for God to help Max find some kind of peace of mind and return to the man she first loved. He now seemed cold most of the time.

The wedding took place as planned in the month of June. They went to a cabin for a week-long honeymoon. Megan told Sara, when she returned that she had never been so lonely in her life. "Max sat quietly most of the time. He did manage to do a bit of writing."

The young bride was happy to return to her job, but her life now was a life of sadness. Max spent hours alone in the den that he had fixed for his writing, leaving Megan on her own nearly all the time. If it had not been for her work she would have gone over the edge, she told one of her friends. Max, by this time had given up all communication with his mother and father again. Megan still had her friends and was determined to keep them. She began doing everything on her own.

Life was beginning to take a new turn. She began to feel nothing for her husband. As her love died, so did her prayers that Max would become a loving and caring partner. She felt that the entire situation was hopeless.

Sara remained in the same lonely state as her daughter-in-law. Spending time with her other two children, was her salvation. She did miss the lack of communication with Max. He was her favorite child, but now he was gone from her for good, or so she thought.

Just as Christmas was closing in, Megan decided to call her mother-in-law and invite her for lunch. They met at a café in a shopping mall. They talked mostly about old times and the problems that seemed almost constant between the father and son.

Megan begged Sara to tell her what happened to cause the ongoing rift between them. After a great deal of prodding, Sara began to tell her about a secret that had remained in the family for many years.

She began by saying, "you must not repeat this to anyone, as we have kept it from our children all these years." With that, Megan promised she would never repeat a word. As Sara began, she pulled out a handkerchief and wiped the salty tears that ran freely down her cheeks. She spoke in a shaky voice telling Sara how John had fallen deeply in love with a co-worker and desperately wanted a divorce so he would be free to marry the woman. It was at that time that Sara told her husband that she was expecting another baby. John was livid. When Max was born he blamed him for ruining his life. Sara went on to say that when the other woman found out about the baby she immediately abandoned John. The anger he felt toward Sara and her baby was out of control. Feeling such despair at the knowledge that her husband had been unfaithful, she prayed for a way out of the marriage. It seemed impossible at the time. They remained together in the home. The love had vanished. Megan realized by now that her mother-in-law had not resolved the issue. She was still full of hurt and anger. It showed in her voice and her swollen red eyes. She talked on and on about the heartbreaking time. To Sara it was a pain that would last a lifetime, but now she had someone to share it with. There seemed to be no stopping her. She had bottled this up for far too long. Now the dam had burst and all the hostility came flooding out. With every word Sara could feel her heart beating faster and the anger was getting harder to control. "All the years of silence had been the hardest," she said. Now she had someone who she could trust. "Perhaps now she could heal," she thought. She apologized for her tears. Megan responded by saying in the kindest voice, " mother, you can only cry with those you trust, and I feel complimented that you trust me enough to grieve and cry with me." The two women now shared a bond and a secret. Their friendship deepened in the most profound way in barely two hours in that little café.

Just as the two were leaving they noticed a travel agency next door. "Let's stop and see what they have to offer for trips for over the holidays." Sara said, as she began to giggle. Megan jumped at the suggestion. When they left the office one hour later they had tickets for Mexico and reservations at a first rate hotel. "What have we done?" Megan said, laughing all the while. Sara could not wait to get home and tell John of her plans. "He deserves to be left alone at Christmas." She thought. "I have spent many years alone," She began having a bit of remorse, thinking of her son Max being alone on the holidays, "Oh well," she thought, "how many days and months has Megan spent alone, because of his cold and uncaring ways? She knew her other two children would be fine, they had many friends.

On the runway in Detroit, all Megan and Sara could say was, "I don't believe we are doing this." Megan asked Sara what the other family members thought of her being away at Christmas. "Oh they are great about it," she replied, they said, "it is about time you did something nice for yourself."

The days passed quickly. The two women enjoyed lying in the sun and shopping in the many market squares. They looked absolutely radiant. Megan flaunted a beautiful suntan and Sara looked ten years younger. Both ladies donning new clothes and a big smile, returned to the Metro airport in Detroit expecting to get the shuttle to their car.

Out of nowhere appeared their entire family. Megan and Sara stood there in total disbelief. "What is going on?" They both chanted at the same time. John walked over to Sara and handed her a dozen red roses. With a tear in his eye he told her how much he had missed her and loved her. He continued on by saying, "while you were away, I became ill and was rushed to hospital with a heart problem. It happened the day you left. I tried to call the family, but the only one who had time to help me was Max. I believe it was God's intervention that made this possible. I am so sorry for the all the years of sadness that I caused you and Max. I know that none of this was your fault. Please forgive me. I have confessed all to Max and the family. They have forgiven me. I have asked God for his forgiveness and feel that he has forgiven me as well. I have spent the past week with Max. He was at the hospital every day, and when I returned home he remained at my side. Sara, will you forgive me?" Now he was pleading in a tearful manner. He promised he would make it up to her for all the lonely years.

Megan stood watching and as she turned to Max, he was also holding red roses. He began to apologize for his past behavior and the sadness he had brought about. He begged her to give him another chance. With that she put her arms around her husband and they held each other for a long time. Sara once again feeling the love for Max, whispered under her breath, "God does answer prayer."

"I'm sorry to interrupt all this," Bob said in his jovial voice. " What do you say we all go home? I understand there is a Christmas dinner with all the fixings waiting for us. After all, we are many seasons late."

Tropical Dream

By Dolores Allen

Wanda stood shivering while she scraped the snow from the mailbox trying to pry open the frozen lid. When she finally retrieved the mail she noticed a postcard with palm trees covering the front. She slowly made her way up the slippery driveway to her house. Her hands began to tremble when she saw that it was from Dale. She felt as though the rug had been pulled out from under her.

The sky was dark making ready to unload another mound of white powder. It already had drifted and piled high on the porch and everywhere. Wading through the tall drifts she thought, "why had Paul not plowed the driveway or cleared the walks like he was hired to do?" She had already paid him. Grumbling to herself she said, "can't depend on anyone anymore. What's the world coming to anyway?" Reaching the doorway, she hurriedly stomped her feet on the hard cement porch trying to remove as much snow as possible. She hated snow on her lovely entrance tile. Wanda was always a bit put out when company left puddles on the floor.

After removing her boots she stood staring in the huge mirror that hung in the foyer. It was her favorite with a wide gold frame showing off the most elegant ornate carvings. It looked like it might have been from the 18th century. She knew that this gothic piece of work was old and very expensive. Her grandmother had given it to her ten years before she died. She had several paintings and artwork in her collection that she was proud of, but nothing could compare to this unique piece. Her grandmother told her that the frame had been hand carved by a French craftsman and it was one of a kind.

Standing in front of this masterpiece and looking at her image she managed a smile. With great pleasure she whispered. "Wanda, you have every right to be proud of your accomplishments." With a giggle and self-satisfaction, she proceeded into the kitchen.

Wanda was a dedicated Physician with a compassionate spirit. Everyone said that she had a caring bedside manner. Some called it an inner and outer beauty. Her smile made her patients feel better.

Being a petite girl never stopped her from doing all the hard tasks. She tackled the heavy repair jobs alone. One summer she replaced the shingles on her roof. She depended on no one.

Wanda had strong hands and a set jaw. Her eyes were as blue as the Pacific Ocean. She managed to get her hair trimmed every two weeks. It made her eyes appear even larger. She said it needed to be short because if it grew long it would take too much time away from doing what was really important.

Pulling out the kitchen chair and getting into a comfortable position to read the postcard was done in slow motion. She felt uneasy. "Why would Dale have gone to Hawaii without telling me? We had always planned to go there on our honeymoon so why would he go now?" She questioned out loud.

Dale and Wanda had been engaged for two years, when one day he informed her that he had been transferred to Seattle, Washington. They had always lived on Cape Cod. Wanda could not believe that Dale would accept this promotion without consulting her. He knew that she could never leave her practice. It had taken years to build up to this, and to just let it go was beyond anything she could imagine. Dale begged her to go with him, but she chose to stay on Cape Cod. She opted for a long distance relationship. After much discussion they made an agreement to visit one another at least once a month. After a few months the visits became less and less. The letters were also becoming sparse.

Wanda proceeded to read the postcard. Her eyes followed each line slowly. It began with, "Dear Wanda, I have thought of you so often in the past few weeks. I find it difficult to put in words what I have to say. I must tell you before you hear it elsewhere. I was married two weeks ago and I am on my honeymoon. Her name is Jane. We met shortly after I arrived in Seattle. There was an instant connection. We decided that we should not wait to get married. I hope that you will be happy for me. Please let us always remain good friends. I send my regards. Sincerely, Dale."

Wanda leaned back in her chair staring at the palm trees on the card. She allowed her imagination to take her to this far away place. She could envision the red ball sliding into the Pacific. Everyone said that the most beautiful sunsets were in Hawaii. She could feel the cool trade winds softly caressing her body. The soft sound of the breeze passing through the palm trees whispering, "aloha." The fantasy was sheer joy. "This was supposed to be me lying on the beach with Dale, and not someone called Jane. This was our dream. How could he?" She whispered in a tearful voice.

In her sorrow, she forgot all about the cold weather and her driveway being unplowed. She was consumed with anger. Her disappointment about Hawaii was sending her mind racing. "What shall I do now?" She thought. Quickly she ran to the phone and dialed. The voice on the other end answered, "hello." "Joe, this is Wanda. You have invited me out for dinner several times over the past two years. I was wondering if the invitation is still open?" His reply was instant. Wanda smiled and continued. "How would you like to come to my home for a home cooked meal on Friday evening around 8:30?" Of course Joe jumped at the invitation.

Wanda prepared an exquisite meal and scattered brochures all around the room. "Yes, they were pictures of palm trees and surfers. On the table beside Joe lay a huge glossy of the Sheraton overlooking Diamond Head and the white sandy beach.

It took awhile before Joe became aware of her scheme, but when he did, he pretended not to notice. He chuckled to himself thinking that it was a smart move on her part.

On New Year's eve that same year he presented her with tickets for two to paradise. "I bet you never thought of this, Wanda? But I think it would be a great place for a honeymoon. Don't you?"

A Dark Side

By Dolores Allen

Marvin had a dark side, but it was not disclosed to many. A few people knew the real boy. He managed to keep it well hidden from most. When he was three, he set fire to the kitchen. His mother believed it was accidental, but Marvin's father knew better. At five years old he had enough anger to create total chaos. Nell, his mother, found him to be an amusing child. She laughed at everything he did. His father did not always find him so sweet. John saw something in his son that was cold and untrustworthy.

As time passed and Marvin got a few years older, Nell began getting letters from his teacher telling her some frightening things about Marvin. Nell did not believe a word even though the notes suggested she take her son for counseling. "Who does she think she is?" She would shout to her husband. John began to talk to Nell about sending Marvin to a private school. Perhaps even a school where he could live in. "It is done all the time," John said. "Look at rich folks, they always send their kids to private schools." Nell was not convinced that it was a good idea.

One evening, while the parents were having another discussion about Marvin and school, he stood in the hallway listening. Anger rose, and he became hot and his body began to tremble. "How can they decide to get rid of me just like that?" He thought. "It's my father, he wants to get rid of me. I will show him." Marvin whispered. He shuffled off to bed, and took his anger with him. Lying in bed he could feel it shaking. "Must control myself, but how will I do that?" He thought. "I will make him pay for this dreadful thing that he is going to do to me. He will be sorry that he abandoned me. Mother will never go along with such a decision," he muttered to himself. Marvin was an only child and very spoiled. His grandparents told John and Nell that if they did not do something about this boy soon they were going to have a jailbird on their hands. Nell just laughed, but John agreed with his parents. "He is controlling you, John, and you are doing nothing to prevent it. One day you will regret it." These were truthful words coming from his father, but John did not know what to do about the situation. It seemed every time he tried to correct Marvin, Nell stepped in and prevented it. Disaster was just around the corner and John knew it.

Teen-age years were quickly approaching, and John was beside himself with worry. Marvin was so strong willed he felt that he would never be able to control him now. He had such a difficult time with him in earlier years and the teens were supposed to be even harder, or so he had heard. His son mouthed back at him, and barely had a kind word for either parent.

Marvin was taking on the appearance of Nell's older brother Homer, who was an angry man also. "Could this happen again in the same family?" Nell thought, recalling some of the pain her mother had endured from Homer. She wondered if she was in for the same rough ride with Marvin. She loved her son, but she was unsure if she could handle all these problems.

Late one night, while Nell and John sat waiting for their son to return home from a party, they heard a car door slam. Upon going to the window, they saw a police car sitting in the driveway. Two policemen were talking with someone, but they could not make out who the individual was. It was not Marvin, but who could it be? John turned the porch light on and discovered that it was his next door neighbor. "What's wrong?" He yelled. The policemen moved slowly up the walk. When they reached the bottom step one officer asked John if Marvin was at home. John told him that he had gone to a party and that they were waiting for his return. The next question was, "have you seen Sally, the girl next door? She has been missing for several hours, and her father thinks that she may be with your son. Do you know if this could be true?" John could not answer the question. Marvin had told them very little in the last several months. He came and went as he chose. The officers began writing everything that John was telling them. The neighbor stayed by the police car. He looked like he was crying. "Mike come inside," John shouted. "I am sure Sally is okay." Mike started toward the house and John could see him clearly now. He was crying. "Why do you think Sally is with Marvin?" John asked. "She is always with him. Last week she came home late and her face was swollen, and one eye would not open. She said Marvin did it. We forbid her to see him again, but she did not listen. Her mother and I think that she may be on drugs." John felt such anger toward his son at that moment that he was prepared to disown him. Just then, Nell came to the door, and it was obvious that she had heard the conversation. "Marvin would not do these things!" She shouted at Mike. "Your daughter is lying!" She cried. "Take it easy Ma'am," the policeman said in a soothing voice. "I am not here to accuse your son of anything, I am just trying to find out what has happened to Sally."

When the police officer left, Mike went into his house immediately. He suddenly looked like an old man. Once John and Mike were very good friends, but somewhere along the way they became estranged. Neither man knew or remembered what caused it. Perhaps it was Marvin that caused the rift, John thought. He began to realize how much he had missed Mike over the last few years. Nell and Mike's wife Jane were never close, but then Nell was never close with anyone.

It was a time of remembering for John. Fear that his son may have done something horrible to Sally and reflecting on his own past life was almost unbearable. He sat in the big old easy chair looking at Nell, and for the first time he saw what a disturbed woman she was. He had many unhappy years, but he thought it was mainly because of Marvin. Now he knew it was not just his son. Nell was equally selfish and nasty. She complained about everything. It began early in the morning, and it would continue on into the night, if John would listen. He did learn how to turn her off, therefore he could attain some peace of mind. It was a difficult life. His neighbors felt sad for him, but he was oblivious to his living conditions. He became so accustomed to this way of life he began to believe it was normal. Nell could not even talk about the weather without whining. He began to sound whiny like his wife. One neighbor said, "it must be like a cold, everyone catches it." John had no idea how other people viewed his family situation. He only knew that this woman across the room from him was someone he looked at with distaste. How could he have loved her? Perhaps he never did. After all he was young when they married. He hated where the years had taken him. "Maybe it would be better if Marvin never came home. Yes, better for all concerned." He thought.

John began seeing this overweight woman as a menace. Her unwashed hair was disgusting to him. Mike's wife kept herself so neat, and their house was clean. John had never had a clean home since he married Nell. For the very first time, he knew what hate was. He had these awful feelings for his wife, and son. "I must find a way to get away from this mess," he thought to himself. The plan started to take on a life of its own. He knew that he would find a way to rid himself of this mean spiteful woman. The more he planned the angrier he became. He thought disgusting thoughts.

It was beginning to get daylight and Nell had left the room. John was still waiting by the window thinking his angry thoughts.

Today was going to be a new beginning for John. He started out by looking through the yellow pages for a divorce lawyer. He came upon an ad that sounded perfect for his needs. Next he knew he needed more money to pay for these extras. He would still have to support Nell, and that low life son of his. He ran down the ads for part time work and behold one leaped out at him. He left his full time work at noon, and went to the address that he saw in the paper. Before his lunch hour was over he had the commitment from the employer that he needed. Next he would get an appointment with a lawyer. Step by step he would change his old life and begin anew. John went to visit his parents that night and disclosed to them his new plans. They were elated. "John, we will help you all that we can. We wanted you to do this many years ago, but we did not want to interfere. It is never to late for a new beginning, son," his mother said. She hugged him hard and promised to be with him all the way. John then told them about Marvin going missing. He told them about his fear for Sally, the neighbor's daughter. John's father, Sam, was a quiet man most of the time, but this was not a time to be quiet. "You must tell the police everything you know about your son. Keep nothing from them. Perhaps it will not be pleasant, but nonetheless, they need all the help they can get to find this missing girl. I hope they find her soon, and unharmed."

When John left his parents tidy little bungalow he left with a heavy heart. He was wishing he could stay there with his parents forever, and feel safe. That was the only place in the world that he felt loved and contented. He immediately turned back and bolted in the front door. "Dad, mom, can I move back home with you? I know it will mean many more miles to go to work, but I cannot go back there." His parents stood facing their son, and in a tearful voice they spoke at the same time, "of course son, come on home."

This time he left his parents home feeling joyful. He could not wait to get to his house. Nell was standing in the doorway when he arrived. The anger was written all over her face. "Where have you been? You left work two hours ago. I called and they said you left early. Marvin is still not home, and I am worried sick that something may have happened to him." "Nell I really don't care where he is. I don't care about any of this. I am going upstairs to pack my things. I will be moving out this evening. I am hiring an attorney to file papers for a divorce. You will have to get off your "lazy boy chair," and find a job. Marvin may have to work as well. I am prepared to pay some support, but the house will be sold. The money will be divided equally. My attorney told me that they handle situations like ours in this manner. You are capable of working, and I am tired of being your caretaker and slave. You and Marvin will have to show some responsibility for yourselves. Excuse me, I am going upstairs and please stay out of my way." With boxes in hand, he ran up the stairs to his bedroom. Nell had not shared his bed in many years.

His wife had complained about her illness constantly. She even planned it. She would make unrealistic comments like, "I think I will have a bad day tomorrow." John wondered how she knew a day ahead, how she would feel. He knew it was just one of the many games she played to keep her from participating in everyday life and responsibility. Now he was beginning to feel excitement just thinking that he would not have to listen to that anymore.

When he began running down the stairway he heard a siren. Stopping dead in his tracks he began to shake. Now he feared that something would happen to put his plans on hold. The doorbell rang, and Nell opened the door quickly. A man in street clothes was standing in the doorway asking for Marvin. "He is not here," she said. "I am Detective Barton from the 5th precinct. Your neighbor's daughter went missing last night, and this morning a search team set out to find her. We would like to ask your son a few questions. We understand that he was seen with her last night at a party." "I don't know anything about that," Nell almost shouted, "and don't bother me again." She abruptly slammed the door.

John pushed Nell aside and bolted out the door and down the walk to his car. Nell was standing on the porch screaming at the top of her lungs. "You can't do this to us, where is the money going to come from?" Suddenly she changed, and in an almost pleading voice she begged him to come back. John backed out of the driveway and sped away without looking back. "Today my life will begin again, regardless of what happens I will NEVER return to that house of horrors," he smiled saying the words out loud.

A few days passed and Sally was still missing. Marvin had not returned home either. The police were back and forth by Nell's house every few hours. She was beginning to get very edgy. The neighbors were giving her cold stares. The anger toward John was increasing by the minute.

Only a few days passed, when Nell reached in the mailbox and pulled out a large brown envelope. She knew it was from a lawyer. Her anger reached such a pitch that she actually thought of killing John. Suddenly a horrible thought came into her mind. "Maybe Marvin was capable of murder?"

Being the self centered woman that Nell was, left her with only one concern, and that was the money. She knew that John did not have to pay support until it went to court, upon which time the judge would tell him what his responsibilities were. To her surprise, John continued paying household expenses every week. She feared that it was only a matter of time before that would stop. She would have to find work. How could she find a job when she was unqualified for any type of employment? Life was changing quickly. The worry, about Marvin and money, was keeping her awake night after night.

Life for John was beginning to seem brighter. He was laughing once in while now. He had not smiled in many years. His parents kept him busy. They showered him with love and attention. Things were once again peaceful and happy. Nell, on the other hand was meaner than ever. Her own family began to avoid her. She felt that she had nowhere to turn. She opened the phone book and turned to the yellow pages. There she came across a mental health clinic that was free. She immediately phoned the hot line number, and made an appointment to see someone. She was set up with a young woman by the name of Amy, who had come from a dysfunctional home as well. Nell felt free to talk to her about the abuse in her childhood. Amy could relate to that. After several visits Nell began to change her appearance. She even thought of returning to night classes at a local college. Amy encouraged her and told her that she would help her get started. Nell left the clinic with a feeling of elation. She could not remember ever feeling that before. She still felt sad that Marvin and Sally were missing. She began to attend a nearby church and openly asked for prayers to find Sally and her son. The neighbors also began praying with Nell for their return. Life was changing for the better. The anger that Nell had felt for John was slowly disappearing. "Could this really be happening?" She thought.

John began coming by to give Nell the money directly instead of mailing it. One morning Nell said, "please, come in and have coffee." John was not sure if that was a wise thing to do, but he did step inside. He was shocked. The house was spotless. Nell looked as thought she had lost a lot of weight. She even looked kind of cute, he thought. They sat and drank coffee, and talked a bit about Marvin, but the main topic was Amy and school. Nell was full of chitchat. John was astonished at the change in his ex-wife. The divorce had been finalized and the judge had set out the money that John was to pay. The only thing that was not settled was the sale of the house. Nell said that she was trying to make it look as good as possible for the upcoming sale. John told her not to hurry because he was not in any great need for the money at this time. He explained that he now had two jobs and could keep things going for awhile. Nell was excited to tell him that soon she would be finishing her course, and then she would be qualified for a good paying job. She followed up by saying that when she accomplished this he would no longer need to support her when the house was sold. "I have been doing a lot of thinking John. You have worked hard many years for Marvin and I, so now it is my turn to help out. You will be able to quit your second job. If I had kept up my end you would never have had to work like this all of your life. For this I am truly sorry. I do not expect you to believe me, but it is the truth. I know I have let you down right from the very beginning. Can you ever forgive me? Maybe one day we can be friends again?" John could not believe what he was hearing. "Of course I believe you," he said. "I think we can start being friends now, Nell."

When the graduation of Nell's class took place, John was there. He bought her red roses. He told her that she should not read any special meaning into it, but he felt she deserved them. "I did not want you to be the only one to graduate without roses," he said.

Nell and John began attending the same church. The prayers continued for Marvin and Sally. The search had never ended for the pair. They never gave up hope that one day they would be found alive. Most folks thought that Marvin had murdered Sally and then ran away. But where was her body? Was the unanswered question. It had been a few years since Nell had heard from any of the detectives that had worked on the case. She knew that they had not put it to rest, because Sally's parents kept her informed.

Nell's new job was working out very well. She began feeling a sense of worth. She felt valued by her employers. The money was more than she had expected. She wanted to share the good news with John. One Saturday night she called John's parent's house, and asked if she could talk with John. His mother was very kind on the phone. She spoke in a concerned manner asking Nell how she was doing. Nell felt tears well up in her eyes. She did not expect that kind of response. When John came to the phone she told him of her joyful feelings. "Your mother was most kind, I am not sure I deserve it." John told her that she did deserve kindness. "Nell, you have worked extremely hard to get where you are. It was not all your fault in the past either. I could have helped you more if I had taken the time to understand a bit more. We were both so young and inexperienced." Nell thanked John and invited him over for dinner. He accepted immediately.

When John arrived at the house there was a, "for sale" sign on the lawn. "Nell I thought we decided to wait awhile before we sold the house?" "I know," she said, "but I thought it would take some pressure off of you. I do not need this big house anymore. Should Marvin ever come home I will not allow him to move back in the house. He will have to remain on his own. I will never protect him again. I made so many mistakes, John."

When dinner was finished, John helped Nell clean up the kitchen. They found themselves talking and laughing about events that happened at work. It was a joyful evening. John felt at ease in this house for the first time in his life. He noticed the new curtains that Nell had hung. "Where did you buy them?" He asked. She told him that she had made them. He was astonished at this new Nell. Before he knew what he was saying, he asked her to marry him. Nell began to cry. "I cannot do that now, but perhaps in the future. I have many more months of counseling. I don't want to do anything until I am sure that I won't slip back into my old ways." "Well, think about it Nell. We will talk again in a few months, okay?" With that, she agreed.

Promotions began to happen in Nell's work place. Many times she thought she was being overlooked, but right in the midst of her self-doubt her boss came to her asking if she would like a supervisory job. It would mean a huge raise, and better benefits. She was so excited. That evening when she reached her house, she went to the phone before she took her coat off. "John," she nearly shrieked in the phone, "can you come over for supper, I must talk with you." John was pleased to accept. "Is anything wrong, Nell?" He asked. "No, but I do have something to talk with you about."

Nell began to prepare the supper. She made sure everything was tidy before she took a shower. She got dressed in one of her favorite outfits. "It seems as though I have been on a clothes-buying spree lately. I wonder why?" She giggled.

The doorbell rang and she ran to the door. Flinging it open, she expected to see John, but to her surprise there stood Marvin, Sally, and a little girl. The girl looked to be about four or five years old. Shock was the only way to describe her feelings. She started to shake. "Where have you been Marvin? The entire city thinks that you did something dreadful to Sally. What happened?" She welcomed them into the house telling them to sit down and explain where they had been.

The doorbell rang again, and this time it was John. He stood there for a moment without saying a word. Relief was written all over his face. He walked to Marvin and put his arms around him and then he hugged Sally. "Who is this young lady?" he asked. "This is Skya, your granddaughter," Marvin said in almost a whisper. "Father, we went away because Sally was pregnant. We were afraid that we would not be able to get married, if we remained here. I was terrible to Sally, and her parents knew that. They would never have approved of us. I was a bad seed, and I knew I needed help to straighten out. We went to small town in Ontario where they had a mental health clinic. It was there that I received the help I needed. I was a cruel and evil young man. I could not seem to get straightened out on my own. I went so far as to hit Sally the night she told me that she was carrying my baby. I blamed her for not using protection. I knew then that I must do something. Mother, you were no example for me. I was very angry with you for a long time. It looks as though you may have changed as well." "Yes Marvin, I have changed with a lot of help also. Your father and I are divorced, but we have regained a friendship." Marvin went on to tell them how they had spiritual guidance from a church in addition to the help from the clinic. John could not believe what he was hearing. Sally spoke softly saying, "we must go to my parents now and tell them. Our daughter will be five tomorrow, and we did not want to keep her from the grandparents any longer. Please forgive us." Marvin began to weep. He asked his parents to forgive him for all the grief that he had caused. John interrupted Marvin by saying, " If things had not happened the way they did, perhaps your mother and I would still be in the same hopeless situation that we were in before. We have all learned a great deal."

When John and Nell were left alone, after Marvin and Sally went to her parent's house next door, they held each other for a long time. John looked into Nell's eyes and smiled an adoring smile. "What was so important that you wanted to talk to me about, Nell?" She almost forgot what it was. "Oh yes," she said, "I got a promotion today. I have been made supervisor. It means a huge pay raise so you need not help me financially anymore." John smiled down at her responding with, "what if I want to? Nell, have you had enough time to think about our situation? My parents think that we should try again, and I feel the same way. I think this time we will succeed. We have both grown up. Look at the changes we have both made. If Marvin and Sally can do it, surely we can. Marvin had such a dark side to his personality, and I would never have thought that he could turn things around, but look at what they have done by working together. Skya is our grandchild. We should begin enjoying her together, as a family. What do you say, Nell?" Just then the door flung open. The neighbors were standing beside the children with great joy on their faces. Nearly shouting, "we are having a celebration! We have a grandchild to prepare a birthday party for so lets get started." Nell began laughing, "that is not all we have to celebrate. John and I have given this a great deal of thought, and we feel that we have learned from our mistakes. We are getting remarried." Skya was jumping up and down in the middle of the floor, but unaware of what was really going on. She knew it must be something great as everyone was smiling and laughing.

Rosie and her Sister

By Dolores Allen

Once upon a time there was a very special girl named Rosie. I know that there are many girls just like Rosie with different names, and from different places. This Rosie looked very much like my granddaughter, Meg. She had big blue eyes that sparkled and deep dimples in her cheeks when she smiled. She smiled most of the time until a sad event happened that took her joy away.

One evening, while she sat watching a Barney movie, her daddy came into the room and turned off the television. He took Rosie in his arms and began by telling her that he was not going to be living at their house anymore. He said that he had lost his love for her mommy, therefore he could not continue to sleep at their house. Rosie sat quiet for a moment as if not to believe what she heard. She began with, "but, daddy, mommy loves you and she won't want you to go." Suddenly she began to cry. Her sister Sadie, was far too young to understand what was happening.

The following morning was moving day and many tears were shed. Rosie and Sadie both cried. Sadie did not know why she was crying, but she did know that she felt anger watching her daddy carry his clothes to the car. Amy was terrified, "what will mommy do without you?" She cried. "What about Christmas and my birthday? Where will you be on Halloween? Please daddy come back, I want you to sleep in your bed."

That evening Rosie's mother took the girls to her grandmother's house.

Rosie rushed into her grandmother's arms wailing, "grandma, daddy in not going to live at our house anymore. I want him to sleep at my house. What can we do to make him come back?" Grandma told her how sad she felt. She promised that she would speak to her father and plead with him to come back home.

The next morning grandma phoned Rosie's dad and begged him to go for counseling with her daughter and try to put the marriage back together. He flatly refused saying that it was definitely over. He said, "he did not love his wife anymore." Soon grandma realized that he was in love with someone else. She gave up talking with him about returning home. She knew that it was hopeless.

The lawyers began making up the agreement. Rosie and Sadie were scheduled to spend every other weekend with daddy and one night a week. It was heart breaking for the girls to have to say good-bye to daddy when their visit was over. When they were with mommy they missed their daddy and it was the same when they were with their father they missed mommy. Rosie would cry at night because she now had only one parent to kiss her good night.

Rosie's father became angry most of the time and she could feel the tension. When he picked her up from school at lunch, he would cry in front of her, telling her how much he missed her. The little girl went into her classroom every day crying. The teachers did not know how to help her.

Rosie and Sadie were becoming a weapon their father was using to hurt their mother. Grandma could not understand why he was so angry? He wanted the divorce to be with someone else. He should have been happy.

One evening quite late the phone rang. When grandma answered her heart sank. She heard her granddaughter on the other end crying. Rosie was pleading for her grandmother to help her. The anger between her parents was destroying her childhood. Being spiritual and a woman of great wisdom, grandma said, "of course I can help. I can pray and ask God to send a healing to your mommy and daddy so they will be able to rethink what they are doing to you and your baby sister. I will pray and ask God to send love into their hearts to take away the anger so it will make life better for all of you. Do you believe that God can do this, Rosie?" She quickly agreed with her grandmother. She always went to church and knew that God was all-powerful, and would never let her down. She would now be able to leave the problem in God's hands like her grandmother said.

"This had been too heavy a load for two little girls to carry all alone and for far too long." Her grandmother also told her that, "every time her parents got angry with one another to start praying. Ask God to forgive them and to PLEASE take away the anger and fill their hearts with love and forgiveness. Tell both of them that if they love you and your sister they will stop. They must use the same energy to give you and Sadie a life that is secure, thus allowing you to have the happy childhood that you deserve. Tell them also that you did not create this unhappiness and that you cannot live in this unhappy home. Can you remember all that? Will you let me know how it goes, Rosie? I will keep in touch."

After several weeks had gone by and many prayers, God came to Rosie's parents in a dream. When they awoke they felt suddenly different. They felt a love that they had not felt in a long time. The anger was gone and all their thoughts were happy. They felt like saying kind things about everyone. It was surely an awakening. God was answering a little girl's prayer.

Rosie learned many lessons during this time and the one most important was that the real Father is one in heaven. He is the one she must rely on for all her needs. Sometimes the father on earth makes mistakes as well as the mommy, but the heavenly "Father, GOD" never makes mistakes and will always love us no matter what we say or do. He is a generous "God." He teaches us lessons like …how to forgive, how to be patient, how to love, how to be honest, and so many more things that we cannot always learn from our earthly parents.

Rosie's mother has moved on and married a wonderful man who loves the girls. Their father has found a peace and joy in his relationship. Now that the anger is gone they can truly enjoy everyday with their little ones. Grandma is happy because "God" came through once again.

Rosie and her sister are now enjoying the happy childhood that they so rightfully deserve. "Amen."

This story is a reminder for all of us who have divorced, thus creating chaos for our little ones.

Pole Hill

By Dolores Allen

It was a lonely Saturday evening when Debbie's friend called to invite her to a singles fellowship evening. She promised that all of the attendants would be Christians. Debbie was a very spiritual woman. She told her friend Sue, that she was not up to going to anything like that and that she had no interest in meeting anyone. Sue responded with, "okay, stay here in your self-pity. Debbie, you are alone because you choose to be. Please start getting out and meeting people. You don't need to feel alone any more. I know you have had one bad relationship, but this does not mean you have to wither up and die. You are far too young to call it a day." Mary began to smile. Suddenly she jumped up and with a flit of her hand, she asked, "can you wait for an hour. I can be ready by then?" "Gladly," laughed Sue.

In another village, not many miles away a man, by the name of "Bill," sat watching the news. It was dreadful news. "How depressing," he muttered out loud. With that he turned the television off and began to read the paper. An "ad" popped out at him. He hurried through it. It said a singles meeting was being held in a small town nearby. He began to think crazy thoughts. "People will think I am wife hunting if I go there. Oh, I don't care what they think, I am tired of sitting here night after night alone. I'm going." Looking at his image in the mirror made him realize the loneliness actually showed in his face. His health could be better too. "What if he did find someone to love and then he became ill?" Many things were running through his mind.

"Stop it! Stop thinking crazy thoughts, I am not interested in a commitment of any kind. I have been alone for too many years. I could never live with anyone, just too set in my ways, I suppose. I just want someone to talk to." After arguing with himself for fifteen minutes, he got ready and rushed out the door.

Bill was in his truck when he remembered he had not put on his after-shave lotion. "Where would it be?" He wondered. He had not worn any in years. Tonight he felt the need to feel and look good. After a wee bit of searching he found it in the back of a cabinet. He sniffed to see if it was still good. Trying to remember the last time he has used it was impossible because it had been too long ago. It still smelled good. The scent did not bring back any special memories. With one last look in the mirror, and a few liberal dabs of calogne he stood smiling at himself whispering, "maybe you still got it. You don't look so bad for a man your age." Another side of him was saying. "Stop it! Stop thinking silly thoughts. Put this nonsense out of your head." Back out the door he scurried and with great speed he backed down the driveway heading for the little town that held great promise.

Debbie and Sue were just arriving when the pick up truck pulled in beside them. Bill could hear Debbie say to Sue; "I can't go in there." "Yes, you can," uttered Sue. "You are coming in and you are going to enjoy the company and the refreshments." Bill was having second thoughts as well. He stopped and adjusted his hat and shuffled in the sand for a moment. He approached the two women that were arguing in the parking lot and asked if he could go in with them. He said he felt strange going in alone. Debbie forgot her negative thoughts and responded to Bill with a smile. "Of course we can all go in together. It is easier that way. Is this your first time here?" "Yes," he replied, "I was very nervous about coming here, but I decided it was better than watching bad news on television. One gets tired of sitting alone watching the boob tube." Debbie and Sue both quickly responded with, "I know what you mean."

The trio entered the huge room. It exhibited warm country decorations with vibrant colors. Every table had real flowers with fancy table clothes. Hanging from the ceiling were triangle shaped silver and gold ornaments that turned with the breeze. They cast beautiful shadows on the walls and ceiling. The trio noticed that everyone was dressed in their finest outfits. They could see, from the doorway, that everyone was laughing and having so much fun. In one corner sat a karioke machine. One couple was standing in front of the machine singing "Unchained Melody." People were sitting around tables drinking coffee. Several came to greet them, and before an hour had passed they knew everyone in the room. Many people had been coming to the club for months and developed good friendships. No one had bonded so tightly as to become a married couple, or if they had, no one knew about it.

The evening went on and they played a few games. Snacks were brought out and many of the ladies baked cookies and fancy cakes. The men made sandwiches. Bill, was unaware that they did this. He vowed that he would do the same next week. All ready he was planning to revisit the club. Debbie was having the same thoughts in her head. She was planning to bake her favorite cookie recipe. When the evening was nearly over, Bill asked Debbie if he could drive her home. He said he felt the need to talk. She quickly responded with, "Yes, but I must tell you that I am not interested in anything more than just friendship, therefore do not get any ideas. Bill replied, "I feel the same way."

Sue was smiling as Debbie approached her in the middle of the room. "Sue would you mind if I drove home with Bill? He seems so lonely and would like to talk for awhile." Debbie hugged Sue, and off she went out the door, smiling and waving at everyone as they left.

The couple walked to the locker room located just outside the main hall. Bill helped with her coat. He took her hand as they left the club. "Debbie, I hope you don't mind driving in a pick-up truck, but that is what I have for transportation." She giggled like a schoolgirl while climbing into the cab of the truck. Bill got in and started the motor, but before he began to drive he turned to Debbie and looked deeply into her eyes, and with a misty look, he told her that she had the most beautiful eyes he had ever seen. He said he felt like they had always known one another. He reached over and placed his hand on hers. She felt the warmth and began hoping he would not take his hand away. "Debbie, can we go for a little drive before I take you home? I know a quiet spot where we can talk and not be disturbed." Debbie nodded her head in agreement.

Driving up the long lonely road with trees on either side it gave a feeling of solitude and peace. The night belonged to them. They wondered where all the cars were. There was no one on the road and it seemed as though they owned the entire county. Chugging up the long narrow winding roadway gave them plenty of time to chat. It was not long before Debbie saw the sign

"POLE HILL." She had heard of people going there to talk and perhaps do a bit of courting, but she had never been here. Bill confessed he had never been there either. He turned the motor off and in the distance they could hear coyotes fighting. Crickets were making their dreadful sound. The frogs were chugging from the ditch beside the road. It was a mournful sound. Debbie ducked quickly as a bat flew in front of the window. Bill reached over and held her for a moment. "Don't be afraid, they can't hurt you. Have you been hurt in the past? Tell me about it." Suddenly she felt the need to tell Bill all about her sad life and disappointments. He held her and comforted her and then it was his turn. Feeling that he could be open and honest with her, he began to share his past. For the first time he had met someone that would understood. He knew already that she cared. They talked about their childhood and failed marriages. They shared sad times and happy times.

As the hours went by, they found that they had the same sense of humor. They laughed at the simplest things. Neither had laughed much in the past several years. They brought out the best in one another. Bill slowly leaned over and kissed Debbie on the cheek and she returned the kiss. Before they knew it they were holding each other not wanting to let go. A flash of light from the side window and a loud knock startled them. "What is that?" they shouted. They could see nothing but the bright light. When Bill opened the door, he realized it was a police officer. Everyone started to laugh. The policeman laughed harder than anyone. He said, "I thought it was teen-agers up to no good. Carry on what ever you were doing." "We were just talking," Bill replied. Debbie became nervous and asked him to drive her home. He obliged and they left Pole Hill, leaving behind many good memories. This was not the last time they visited Pole Hill. They returned many nights, after the club meetings ended and talked until the wee hours of the morning.

Debbie and Bill knew that there was a very strong attraction, but both agreed that they did not want a commitment of any kind that would spell marriage.

Cold weather was closing in and the friendship grew to the point that they were doing everything together. They attended church hand in hand and both families were becoming a part of the picture. Bill was finding it harder to say good-bye. Although Debbie did not want to admit it, the feelings were mutual. She still had many fears. Her past was not buried. She knew she had a great deal of healing to do. Bill, on the other hand seemed to have come to terms with his past and was ready to move on. He was afraid to tell Debbie how he felt, thinking she might back off, then that would end their relationship.

One evening Debbie cooked a lovely dinner for her dear friend. After they cleaned up the kitchen they sat down to watch a movie. It was a love story and throughout the movie they heard the word, "soul mate" several times. When the movie was over Debbie leaned toward Bill and whispered softly, "I believe with all my heart that we are "soul mates." I have been holding back, but I am willing to take a chance if you are. I trust you completely." He held her tight and began to weep, then reaching into his pocket he pulled out a beautiful diamond ring. "I have been carrying this for months, waiting for the opportunity to ask you to marry me. I believe with all my heart that you are my soul mate. I cannot imagine living the rest of my life without you. I want you by my side for always. Please say you will marry me." Debbie began to cry. He gently brushed her tears away. The answer came tearfully. "Yes! I want to marry you. I feel we were meant to be. Some divine power has put us together and God will protect us and keep us joined in peace and happiness forever." Bill could not contain his excitement. He was a quiet man by nature, but not this night. He jumped up and shouted, "Debbie! I love you! I always will!" They were laughing so hard through their tears that they may have been heard throughout the county.

They became husband and wife in front of many friends and family. When Pastor Don uttered the words. "Until death do us part" there was not a dry eye in the church. They knew that God had joined them together forever.

Merry Christmas

By Dolores Allen

"Counting pills." Alice barked as she prepared for bed. "Tired of taking pills. Wonder if all old people have to take as many pills as we do? No wonder the world is so upside down. All we ever do is take pills and run to doctors." Ernie sits rocking and scoffs at his wife's remarks. "You say that every night, Alice. I am sick and tired of your whining and complaining. Can't you ever say anything positive?" Alice moves close to the bedroom door, but decides to sit for awhile before going to bed. "Wish the rain would stop," she grumbles. "It ain't rainin," shouts Ernie. Alice is quick with a comeback. "Put your hearing aid in and maybe you could hear the rain. Maybe, if you wore it once in awhile you wouldn't be contradicting me all the time. You might hear what I am saying." The old man rattles the newspaper and shows his anger by turning the pages in a flurry. "Why are we arguing all the time?" He asks his wife of 50 years. "Perhaps it is just a habit," she replied.

"Have you noticed the couple that sits in front of us in church? They are always smiling at one another and they never seem to be angry. Maybe we should go to a different church. Maybe that would help get rid of the anger." Ernie mutters. "It can't be the fault of the church. The couple that sit in front of us go the same one and they seem happy." Alice said in a stern voice. "Well, whose fault is it then, Alice? Oh, just go to bed and stop with the arguing!" Alice shouts back with fury, "don't tell me what to do."

The old couple were both veterans from the Second World War and had received many medals to show for their courage. They were both in a command position during those years and learned early on how to bark the orders. They found it difficult to be civil with one another, and after a few years, it became impossible.

Ernie wants to talk about the past and barely remembers any names, places or events in the right order. He tries to rely on Alice to help him. This is a hopeless assumption because Alice remembers less than Ernie. When she does try to help him, he contradicts every word. One minute silence... the next combat. Alice talks constantly about sickness, and other people's problems. This has managed to turn all their friends away. They now sit alone, day after day, and wonder why no one ever calls or visits.

They are not alone. Another couple just down the street sits alone talking about their pills and pains. They discuss the health of Alice and Ernie. They are convinced that their pain is greater. Elwood and Bea are a couple of copycats. They want to make sure that they take as many pills as their neighbors. Having raised a good family, and being financially secure, they still whine and jaw about what they don't have. Happiness eludes them as it does the couple down the street.

Alice and Ernie had one son. He was the apple of their eye. Ernie Jr., graduated from a community college, but could not find work nearby. Not wanting to leave home, he remained with his parents until his end. Jr. was easily led. Well, that was what his parents said. "He would never have been involved with drugs and all that bad stuff if others had not enticed him. It was all their fault," Alice said. She vowed that she would never forgive those no good pushers for killing her son. Her husband felt the same way about it, and each day increased his anger. The elderly couple endlessly grieved their boy. The only thing that broke the silence in the home was the arguments and constant complaining.

Alice grumbles, "I suppose it will soon be snowing, and we won't get out anywhere." "We never go anywhere now," Ernie retorts. " What will be different when the snow comes?"

"Wonder how Bea and Elwood were so lucky to have three children that all turned out so good? We were better parents than they were. Do you think God favors them?" Alice asks in her whiny voice. "Of course, God favors them. How do you think that they got the money to educate those kids, and go on all those vacations, if God didn't favor them? We have just been unlucky." The old man shouted from the across the room. "I can't take any more of your cranky behavior," snorts Alice. "I am going to bed." With that she turns and heads down the hallway to her bedroom. "How many years has it been since you moved out of our bedroom?" Her husband asks. There is no reply.

"Oh well, I may as well turn the television on and watch the news," Ernie mumbles to himself. "Why in the world are they playing a Christmas movie this early? Hunting season is not even over, so it can't be that close. Well, I guess maybe it is. I might as well watch a bit of it before the news begins. I suppose Alice will start nagging about Christmas and all the extra work very soon. That ought to be fun."

"I wonder how the widow next door has time to entertain so much company? She works so many hours and with three children to raise on her own. I don't know how she manages. She is always laughing and seems to be so contented." He continues his solo conversation with, "here I go talking to myself again, at least I don't argue with myself," he chuckles.

On the screen Jimmy Stuart is yelling at his family and running out the door. The last thing Ernie remembers was the actor on the bridge getting ready to jump, and saying how he wished that he had never been born. "This is the way that I feel most of the time." Ernie murmured. "Such a sad movie. I don't think that the title, "It's a Wonderful Life," is a good title for this movie. On second thought, I guess it don't much matter. It is sad like my life. Wish an angel that needed wings, would come to me and help me get my life straightened out."

His mind goes back to the widow next door, "wonder if she has a boyfriend? She sure doesn't seem lonely. How can some folks have so many people in their lives and we remain so alone? It must be Alice's fault. I know that people like me. Yes! It is Alice that is keeping people away. I wish that I had never laid eyes on that woman."

"What happened to the news? Is it over? I missed it entirely. Must have fallen asleep. I may as well go to bed. No use sitting here just waiting to die," he whispers. The old gentleman meandered down the hall stopping to look in on Alice. He soon discovered that she was not in her room. "Where could she be? She is not in the bathroom, could she have wandered outside in the cold?" Ernie donned his coat and hat and rushed outside, in a panic. "Alice," he shouted, "where are you?" There was no reply. He went next door to the widow's house. "Have you seen Alice?" He asks in a frightened voice. "No," she answers, "but I will put my coat on and help you look for her." "I fell asleep on the couch after she went to her room. I was watching the movie where Jimmy Stuart was on the bridge saying, "I wish that I had never been born." I knew how he felt. I was wishing that I had never laid eyes on Alice when I fell asleep. I didn't mean it, and now I am afraid that she may be gone from me forever. What have I done?" He sat holding his head in his hands. Now the old man was beginning to weep. The widow told him not to over dramatize, that Alice would be found.

They began calling neighbors to see if anyone had heard from Alice. The reply was always the same. Ernie began to pray and ask God to help him find Alice. He began to repent for the unkind words that he had spoken over the years. He asked God for forgiveness and promised to stop blaming everyone for his loneliness and sadness. He begged and pleaded and with shaking hands he headed for the door. The widow promised that she would continue to look for his wife. With shoulders drooping, and eyes swollen nearly shut, he went home.

Upon reaching the house, he noticed he was not wearing his glasses. "Must have left them in the bedroom. I must call the police and get them looking for Alice." He found his missing glasses on the dresser. He placed them on the end of his nose and looking over them, he reached for the light in the corner of his room. Much to his surprise, there lay Alice on his bed. "Where have you been?" She asked? "I have been waiting for you. I thought it was about time we started to live again instead of counting pills and complaining all the time. Ernie, you were right when you said we have been grieving our son far too long. We have both been just waiting to die instead of dying to live. I have been a cantankerous old woman. My complaining all the time must have been very hard to take. Lets start over and stop blaming God and everyone for our loneliness." She went on in a breathless manner by saying. "I have an idea, let's have Bea and Elwood and their family for Christmas dinner." With out hesitation, Ernie almost shouted, "Yes! And we can invite the widow and her children from next door. Enough feeling sorry for ourselves. Lets be thankful that we have the money to buy the pills to keep us going. We have so much to be grateful for! So let's start counting our blessings and stop focusing on our woes." Alice was in total agreement. "No more arguing over petty things, and that is a promise." Ernie stood looking down at Alice with a big smile on his face. "Can I lay down beside you Alice? I still love you." The old woman reached for her husband and with a twinkle in her eye she whispered, "of course Ernie. I have one question for you. What would you like for Christmas?"

Nora's Tragic Mistake

By Dolores Allen

Nora sat, holding Alex clutched to her large bosom, rocking as if in tune with the wind. The cold north gale wind was making sounds that Nora had never noticed before. It became almost a rhythm in her mind. Why had Rob not returned home on their son's birthday? He had promised that he would, but then he did not keep too many promises. She knew in her mind that Rob was not the caring father that she had hoped he would be for her son. It was nearly dusk and the wood was running low. "Must have enough on hand to keep away the chill until morning," she thought.

Another one of Alex's birthday's had come and gone without his father being present. There were no presents or balloons like most four-year-olds had to enjoy. No friends or candy, no cake, or ice cream. Nora could feel steamy hot tears running down her cheeks and did nothing to dry them. Alex lay with his face buried in his mother's warm sweater.

Nora was a pretty woman, with a somewhat large frame. Her cheeks were rosy with high cheekbones. A large dark mole was noticeable just under her left eye. Some called it a beauty mark. This added character to her strong face.

Nora grew up in the Saskatchewan prairies, and married Rob at an early age. In just a few short months after their wedding, Rob had an opportunity to work in a logging camp in northern Alberta. Nora did not wish to go and leave her father. She was with child at the time, but she did believe

73

her first responsibility was to go with her husband. She packed hastily one chilly night while Rob prepared the wagon that would take them to the train station.

It was nearly midnight when Rob finally had the wagon prepared. Upon entering the cabin he noticed that Nora was crying. He leaned over to kiss his wife good night. "It will be okay Nora, we will earn more money. Then, when we return, we will have saved enough to build a good house and have good food. You will not have to worry anymore." "But Rob, I will be alone when the baby comes. There are no doctors close to the camp. What will happen if something goes wrong at birth? The baby could die or I might not be able to survive. I am too young to be alone at this time. I know nothing about delivering a baby. You will be far away in the woods and unable to help me." "Hush Nora, there will be plenty of women around to help you. It will be okay. It will only be for a couple of years anyway. Just give it a chance and see what happens. If, for some reason, we cannot make it we will return. Okay Nora?" He reached over and held her close, reassuring her that things would work out and that she would be fine.

Early the next morning Nora packed a lunch and off they went to the station. Bert, Nora's father, drove them to the train in a wagon carrying their belongings. The station was cold and dark when they arrived. The long wait for the train was sad and lonely. Bert decided that he would not wait for the train before starting his ride back home. He unloaded the boxes by the tracks to make it easier for Rob to throw them on board. Nora held her father tight as she kissed him goodbye. Her mother had died when she was a little girl, therefore, Bert was left on his own to raise his daughter. The love he had for her was deep. She returned that love. It was devastating for her to leave him. She knew her husband must come first. They sat for an hour listening to the wind howling around the old rundown station house. Finally they heard a faint whistle in the distance.

After throwing their belongings on board they felt a great relief setting foot on the train steps. They entered what they thought would be a warm passenger car with soft cushion seats. It did not come up to their expectations. The car was cold and the frost on the windows was inside. The rattle and clanging nearly drove Nora crazy. Fear was setting in, thinking she might lose the baby, from the rough jerking cars and cold floors. Rob went to their luggage and, in a box, he found a small blanket. He wrapped it around Nora's feet. He could see the fear in his wife's eyes. Suddenly he began feeling a terrible guilt. "What am I putting my wife through?" He thought. "Must focus on the positive things and not the harshness of it all. We will have money to give our children a better life than what we had." He muttered to himself.

Riding for many hours on the rickety train was taking its toll. They were snapping at each other and all pleasantries had gone by the wayside. "Is this what married life is going to be like?" Nora thought to herself. Rob growled, "get me another sandwich and a cookie." "They are all gone, we ate them all. The food container is empty." Nora whispered in a nervous tone. Rob retorted in a nasty voice, "You eat too much. You should have rationed them out so we would have enough to last the entire trip. I don't know what you were thinking, woman! You can't do anything right. I suppose it is because you did not have a mother to teach you things like most girls." Nora sat broken hearted. She wished at that moment that she could return to her father, but knew that was impossible.

It was in the wee hours of the morning that the train pulled into the small northern village in Alberta. It was a bitter cold morning. White powder was swirling around making it almost impossible to see more than three feet in front of them. Rob knew there would be a three hour wait before the crew leader arrived to pick them up. "Well, we might as well go inside and see if there is any wood. If there is, I will build a fire to keep us warm while we wait." The door was hanging on one hinge. An old stove sat in the middle of the floor. There was no wood. The couple sat shivering from the dampness and severe cold.

After a short time, Nora could hear a sound in the distance. "I think I hear someone approaching," she said. With that, Rob ran outside. The crew leader was driving a horse pulling a logging sled behind. When he entered the building, Nora could not help noticing that the man standing before her had the kindest eyes she had ever seen. She wondered if he looked that way only because Rob had been so unkind to her on their journey. His name was Tim. He smiled at Nora with softness in his eyes that made her feel that she already had a friend. His eyes lowered to her belly. Suddenly he ran to the sled and got a huge warm woolen blanket and wrapped her, after which he led her to the sled. Rob stood by watching the kind treatment Nora was receiving from this stranger. When Tim wrapped his arms around Nora as he walked her to the sled, she felt a tingle going through her entire body. She had never experienced such a sensation before. She looked into his eyes and smiled which prompted Tim to give her a gentle squeeze. She did not understand the meaning of what was happening, but it felt reassuring anyway. She knew that, whatever it was, she was willing to accept it without question. Each time she looked at Tim, on the ride to the logging camp, she felt fuzzy feelings that were unexplainable.

Upon arriving at the cookhouse, they were greeted with hot coffee and biscuits. Many of the ladies were hovering over Nora and asking when her baby would arrive. All the attention was giving the mother to be "a sense of peace." She was starting to feel a bit more secure knowing that she had people who would help her when the delivery day came.

A stone faced man came into the cookhouse beckoning Rob and Nora to come with him. He was about to show them their living quarters. Nora did not want to leave the warm kitchen and the steaming coffee. She knew that she should go and see where they would be living for the next couple of years.

Many of the ladies in the camp were older. The men wore heavy beards. Haircuts seemed to be out of the question. Tim was the only one who had nicely trimmed hair, and a cropped beard. He had a city look. Nora found herself wondering who he really was, and why he was here. He looked as though he did not belong.

Horror is hardly the word to describe the look in her eyes as she entered the dingy room. It was damp and the smell was reeking of dirty clothes. There was no private place to wash or change. A straw tick lay on the floor in one corner. In the center sat an old wooden table with two chairs that had the backs broken. What looked like on old oil barrel with legs was the stove and it sat over in one corner. Hanging on a small window was a piece of burlap. The wind was shifting it from side to side. Nora assumed the window was broken, but it was just large cracks in the frame. Above her head hung a dark frayed rope, which was her clothesline. The floor was hard clay and upon it lay old burlap bags. In another corner, she noticed long spikes in the walls for hanging clothes. All Nora could think of was, "where is my baby going to sleep?" It did not look sanitary enough for a baby to exist in such filthy conditions.

Nora did manage to settle in while awaiting the arrival of her child. As the days, came and went, her fears grew. "Can I survive such misery and still be a good mother?" She kept uttering to herself. She grew up without a mother and wanted to be the best mom ever to her child. Uncertainty was like a hidden monster in a dark closet. She dared not show her feelings. Inside was a horrendous gloom that never seemed to escape. One bitter cold Good Friday, she awoke with a sudden shock. She felt a dampness under the blankets and an earth shattering pain in her back. "This can't be the baby coming because the pain would be in my belly," she thought. She did not get up or try to call anyone for help thinking that if she remained quiet it would go away. Remaining on the floor, in the stressful situation, for about an hour, was all that she could tolerate. When she could not stand the suffering any longer she decided to go to the cookhouse and ask for help. Trying to get off the straw tick was impossible. She could not get up. Screaming for help was an effort, but she continued to yell. Suddenly the door opened wide and the bright sunlight shone through. Because of the bright glare, she had a difficult time making out who it was. When she heard the voice she knew it was Tim. " Help me," she cried. He entered the room and held her in his arms. Comforting her, he told her he would get help. She begged him not to leave her. He stayed by her side and delivered the child. He then proceeded to wash the baby boy. Turning to face Nora and holding the newborn, he gave her the warmest smile. Walking slowly to the bed where Nora lay, he laid the infant in her arms with such tenderness. She wept and thanked him for his kindness.

Together they lay looking at this wonderful miracle that God had created. Tim felt as though this child was his. He began to weep. Nora embraced the child, and Tim. "Please Tim, tell me about it. What is so painful for you? I know that you do not belong here any more than I do. What happened to bring you here?" Tim began in a mournful sound saying, "Nora, I have suffered great sorrow. I was married to a wonderful girl and we were very happy. We were eagerly awaiting our first child. The room was ready and the clothes were in place on the cradle. Mary and I would sit and look at the empty cradle each night just waiting for our child to arrive. One night it all came to a sad conclusion. I had to go to another city for some supplies for the store where I was employed. Upon arriving home the next day I came to a pile of ashes. The house had burned and Mary could not get out. She must have been in a sound sleep. They said it looked as though she may have failed to close the door on the stove. The coals must have fallen to the floor and started the fire. My life was over... or so I thought. I decided to leave the bad memories behind and come up north to work. Here I am, and now I am happy that I came. Thank you Nora for listening to me. I have told no one here what happened. I did not feel like answering questions. I felt that if I did not talk about it, perhaps the pain would go away. The grieving has not stopped. I do feel better sharing it with you." Slowly he got up and walked to the door. "Good-bye for now Nora, I will send a couple of ladies in to help you."

Looking down at this newborn was an earth moving experience for Nora. Her husband would not arrive until the next evening from the woods. She wondered if he would be as happy about the baby as she was, or, would he be just be as cranky as ever? Oh well, at least she had Tim for a friend. He always helped out in a time of need.

Saturday morning Nora got out of bed and warmed water to wash herself and the child. She put on a nice flowered dress. She wanted to look her best when Rob arrived. She dressed the baby in a flannel suit with a home knit sweater and booties. He looked so beautiful laying there by the stove in the wooden box that Tim had made for a cradle. When night was drawing near the door flung open. Rob stood glaring at Nora with a coldness she had never experienced before. He had been ugly, but never this angry. "How could you let a man help you deliver our child? I stopped at the cookhouse and the women there told me that Tim delivered my son. How could you? You are a disgusting woman and I will never trust you again." Nora begged and pleaded for Rob to understand. She explained over and over again how it all happened, but he would not relent. He left her there alone and shattered. He did not return that night. Some say he was in the bunkhouse with another lady whose husband had not returned for the weekend. Many of the men stayed in the field for days not returning to the quarters because of the distance.

Rob came back in the late afternoon on Easter Sunday. He informed Nora that he was leaving to go back to the woods. He did not look at his son or kiss his wife good-bye. He just left in a flurry. Nora could smell liquor on his breath.

Weeks and months went by and Nora rarely heard from her husband. If he left the woods, she was unaware of it. She had little to eat most of the time and, when she did eat, she felt sick. After two years of suffering, Rob came to her and told her that they were moving further up north in the woods. There was a nice cabin where they could live. He said he would make more money and the time was drawing near for them to return home to Saskatchewan. He vowed he had a great nest egg saved, and that they would have it easy once they returned to the prairies. Nora was excited and happy to go to the new cabin. She longed for home and anything that would speed up their return was okay with her. Packing up was easy and off they went.

The cabin was in a very secluded spot in the woods. Rob was gone for days and when he did return he brought very little food. Nora was losing weight and their son Alex was small for his age. Nora told Rob that they must return home before Alex was ready for school. It was such a lonely life for Alex. He had no playmates or any of the things that Nora had promised herself that she would give her child. He was far worse off than she had ever been. As time passed Rob was coming to the camp less. Once in while he would send food by one of his fellow workers.

Sitting here rocking and waiting for Rob's return for their son's birthday was a time of sadness. She began recalling all of the disappointments that she had experienced in her short marriage. It felt many times like she had been married for 100 years. The suffering had gone on forever. It had only been five years, but it was an eternity for Nora. She now knew for sure that Alex's father would not return for his birthday. She wondered if he even remembered it was his birthday.

The cabin was getting colder by the minute. Nora began to think it would be better for both her and her son if they just sat there and froze to death. Life had no meaning any more. There was no way of returning to her father. "Yes," she said in a firm loud voice, "my mind is made up. I will let the fire go out. It will be peaceful." With that decision, for the first time, since she left her father, she found a "sense of place." "No more suffering or going hungry or having birthdays without your father." She whispered in her son's ear. Peacefully, Nora and her son drifted off into a deep sleep.

With a loud bang early the following morning the door burst open and there stood Tim with two ladies from the cookhouse. "Are you okay, Nora?" Shouted Tim. "Yes!" Nora whispered. "Get your things together we are taking you back to the camp, and then you are going home. We have bad news. Rob was found frozen to death outside a barroom in one of the camp villages. He has been going there every weekend and drinking. They believe that he was drunk, fell down and could not get up. The coroner said he must have fallen asleep after he fell. Nora I am sorry to have to tell you this, but the good news is that you can now go back to your father. This is no place for any woman. It is hard for strong men to survive. Many of the ladies have already left the other camps and the few remaining will leave soon. I will accompany you to your fathers." Tim continued talking to Nora in a much softer voice now. He knelt before her and put his arms around her and her child. With tears in his eyes he whispered gently, "can I take care of you and your son? Nora, I love you and have for a long time. In my mind Alex is already my son. Will you allow me to be his father, and take care of you both? We could marry right away. It would be the best for both of us. We could return to the prairies as husband and wife. What do you say, Nora?" Holding Tim tightly she whispered, "YES" in such a confident voice. "I promise I will make you happy, Nora. Your suffering is over." Tim sobbed the words. The ladies stood by watching the drama unfold with the most delightful looks. Nora wondered how only hours before she was willing to allow herself to end it all. Now she felt only joy and happiness. She whispered a silent prayer asking God to forgive her for entertaining such a destructive thought.

Nora, Tim, Alex and baby Sarah are living in a small village just outside of Regina, enjoying a peaceful life. Nora's father is a frequent visitor and his grandchildren are having the lifestyle they deserve. Oh yes, Alex is a grade "A" student and their daughter Sarah has inherited Tim's good looks and Nora's kind spirit.

A New Family

By Dolores Allen

Jeffrey lay in his crib with his face scrunched up and tears running down his cheeks. He had become aware that when he cried loud enough the lady would come, but, only after a long time of waiting, to remove his wet clothes. His clothes were soaked from his bottom and nearly reaching his neck. The discomfort was more than he could bear. His world was almost silent. He could hear a faint, "shut up" when the caretaker did eventually come to change his wet napkin.

If only he could fall asleep and not feel the burning on his flesh. Suddenly, the lady in charge was staring down with eyes as cold as steel. Her mouth was hissing. The spray from her mouth covered his face. The faint sound of "shut up' was a sound he thought might soon bring dry clothes. Jeffrey had been waiting, for what seemed like hours, for Elsie to take care of his needs. She pulled the wet clothing off in a rough manner and glared into the face of this little boy with such distaste that even a baby understood the hate. His body was covered with sores and scars from negligence.

Elsie was cold as stone. The neighbors said she was born heartless, so why did the Children's Aid allow her to take care of these helpless children? Her husband was as unkind as she, and gave no words of encouragement to any of the children in their keeping. Money was the only motive that they had for keeping these abandoned children.

Elsie was a big woman with dark hair that was rarely combed, and her husband Wendell was just as slovenly. Neither of the pair could talk without yelling and cursing. The Children's Aid rarely investigated, therefore, they did not know of his plight. The conditions that the youngsters lived in were absolutely abhorrent. Neighbors rarely saw the children, hence, they were unaware of the abuse so they did not report the situation. Many nights the foster children went to bed hungry.

Jeffrey was the only child in Elsie's care at this time, and still she was neglectful of him. He was given the bare necessities. There was no love or tenderness that is so important in child rearing.

When spring arrived, it was just around the time of the young lad's first birthday. A young girl entered his room where he spent most of his days and nights. She picked him up and hugged him. The look on her face was a look he had never seen before. It was a smile. He knew it was a kind look, not like the looks he got from Elsie. The young girl put his hand on her face and moved her lips to spell Judy. She was a godsend to Jeffrey. This little boy hung on tight, touching her face. She reached down into the crib and hugged him. He hugged her back. "Who was this person with such a kind heart?" He wondered. She made no sound that he could hear and she smelled so good. Her hair was golden, and she had blue eyes that sparkled. She had the softest hands and face. He could not stop caressing her cheeks.

The next morning he awoke early and hoped that he would see her again. By noon, Judy entered his room once again and he began shaking all over. Excitement was giving him shivers. He could not stop kicking and squirming until she picked him up and began hugging him. This day she sat and rocked him and made lip movements. He could not hear, but he knew they were soft kind sounds and not the, "shut ups" he had heard faintly in the past. Jeffrey snuggled to her breast. He hoped that she would never put him down. He knew nothing of angels, but what he did know was that she was someone sent to protect him.

When Jeffrey had reached the age of two, Judy was still a frequent visitor. Other children his age were larger and accomplished in the simple tasks like dressing themselves, etc. He was far behind even though Judy was trying hard to teach him. He still spent most of his time in the bedroom and Elsie never did enter the room when Judy was there. This did seem strange, but Jeffrey did not mind as he had her all to himself. He learned to whisper, "Judy."

One day when he was laying in a dirty bed, he kept whispering, "Judy,

Judy." Elsie entered the room and began screaming her regular, "shut up!" She could understand what he was saying and wondered if Judy taught him how to speak. She knew no one else had been there to teach him. "How could he have learned that word?" She sputtered, "He is deaf." Tears began running down Jeffrey's cheeks. He longed for Judy to come. He lay waiting and waiting, but, when nightfall came, Judy had not appeared. Had Elsie sent her away?

Days, weeks, and months passed. Judy never returned to Jeffrey. Had this been just a dream or was she an angel sent to him when he most needed comfort?

Soon Jeffrey was nearing school age. He had not learned many basics required for a first year student. He could not talk or hear and the school was not equipped for such a handicapped child. Playing in the park was not allowed. He rarely saw other children. He did not have any idea how to interact with others. Elsie and her husband remained cold and uncaring. The young boy was not allowed to go to a specialized school for the deaf. He continued to live in silence and alone.

Early one morning, a fancy car drove up in front of the house and a woman slowly got out carrying a briefcase. She stopped and looked around the yard. After seeing the messy condition of the area where Jeffrey had to play she proceeded up the steps to the porch. She was unaware that the boy was rarely allowed out in the yard. Jeffrey could see her from his bedroom window. She looked vaguely familiar. When the lady entered his room he felt as though he had met her before, but he thought it was probably one of his dreams. She looked like Judy. Jeff had learned by this time that Judy was probably not even real, but only in his mind. Suddenly the visitor lifted his shirt and saw the scars on his back. She then lowered his trousers and found more scars. Jeffrey recognized friendly eyes and reached over and hugged her. The lady responded and held him for a long time. Elsie looked on in her cold-hearted manner. The ladies name was not Judy, but Amber.

It looked to Jeffrey as though she might be having a heated discussion about him. He could not hear, but the looks were looks he was all too familiar with. "I wish I could hear so I would know what was going on. How come others hear things and I can't?" He thought. Amber sat and wrote on many papers. Then she proceeded to file them in her briefcase. When that was completed she abruptly left the house. Jeffrey felt the salt water running down his cheeks again. "Why did she have to go?" He thought. Judy left and now Amber. How he wished she would take him with her.

A few weeks had passed and Jeffrey was sitting on the front porch looking very sad. Silence was all he knew and probably all he would ever know. Looking up the street he saw the same shiny car that Amber drove approaching. He was elated, it was she. Amber ran up the walk and took his hand. She motioned him to get in the car. She yelled something to Elsie, but Jeff did not know what was going on. Amber then opened her car door and quickly got inside. She started down the street at a rapid speed. Jeffrey was full of excitement. Suddenly he was alone with Amber and away from Elsie. "Oh, please let this be forever. I don't ever want to return to that house again!" He thought.

After driving for awhile they reached a huge cement block building with many floors. When they entered a room on the second floor it was filled with strange odors. A man in a white coat came toward them and shook Amber's hand. Jeffrey was ushered into a room and immediately a doctor appeared and put a headset on the boy covering both his ears. This was just one of many tests on Jeffrey's ears to follow. Dr. Brown was a kind and patient man. He never came into the room without giving a wink to the young lad. Whenever Jeffrey looked frightened, he would tickle him and make him laugh. It was a strange laugh, but at last Jeffrey felt that he might be making some sounds. Amber had kept Jeffrey at her home all the while they were doing the hearing tests. He loved sleeping in a clean bed and the food was sooo good. Amber was kind. She took him everywhere with her. He was never alone like he had been at Elsie's house. Never having ice cream before he was now able to have it anytime he chose.

Amber and Jeff made one last visit just before Christmas, and this time he had a cold hard device put in his ear. He could barely believe what he heard. Amber said softly, "Jeffrey, there will be many sounds you will not recognize, but soon you will. I know you will not understand anything I am saying, but I have someone who will teach you. Come with me dear." The young lad was so excited he could hardly contain himself. All these sounds that were coming through, were like magic. He heard a car horn, and, looking below from the window, he heard roaring sound of a huge bus. Children were getting off the bus laughing and screaming and a loud roar from above frightened him. He looked up and a huge helicopter was hovering over head. Tires squealed and he heard people scurrying about chatting. The sounds were deafening. A car passed by with the radio full blast, and somehow he knew that it was music. He did not know how he knew, but he did. He had felt the vibrations before when the radio was loud and he learned rhythm. There were so many screeching sounds. He knew that he would get used to the new world he was now entering. A new world, with no more silence, was waiting for this little boy. He would be able to play and laugh and honk horns and scream like the other children. He was so full of excitement, but the thought of returning to Elsie was sobering. Fear was creeping back. He thought that they would now send him back where he came from since his hearing had be restored with this new device.

Jeffrey and Amber went down the hall and sat in a small room with soft burgundy leather furniture, waiting for someone. He did not know who or what exactly. He began playing with some toys that lay in a box, and when he looked up from the floor he saw Judy. She was real and not a dream or an angel, she was really here. Judy ran to Jeff and held him tight. He melted in her arms. Jeffrey began to weep. For the first time, he heard his own voice. Suddenly he started to laugh at his own wailing, as it sounded so funny.

Judy was Amber's sister and she was trained in teaching deaf children how to talk. She knew sign language and all about the hearing impaired. Now Jeffrey could hear, and he would learn to talk with Judy's help. She knew that he would not understand what was being said, but she told him that he would never have to return to Elsie's house again. She added that he now belonged to her, and that she had adopted him "Jeffrey, I am taking you home with me. My home will be your home from now on." She took the boy by the hand and left the building. Somehow, even though he did not understand the words, this little deaf boy knew that Judy's home would be his home.

My Friend Robbie

By Dolores Allen

Hair blowing in the warm summer breeze, much like a vast ripened wheat field, is one way to begin describing my best friend. Weaving from side to side with each gait, like a graceful young pony and smiling all the time. He looked like a character from an old Norman Rockwell calendar. His cheeks were cherry red, and his eyes were as blue as the sky above. The joy he felt, with every passing day, was something he passed on to everyone who was fortunate enough know him. He was my best friend Robert, but to me he was just Robbie. I can close my eyes and still see him running through the tall grass to my house with his bibbed overalls rolled up to his knees. Many times they were adorned with a patch or two. I gave mention to his hair only because it was soft and yellow and when the sun shone it became even more radiant. That is one of my favorite memories of him as a young lad. Robbie would not want me to describe him in such a fashion as he had a hard time with compliments. He could give them, but had trouble accepting them. His life became a living testimony to many, because of all the hardships he endured in his adult life. He never complained, only moved forward with the same boyish gait.

The sun would hardly have time to poke it's bright yellow head above the horizon when you would see Robbie running down the road with a fishing pole over one shoulder, and an old rusty pail hanging over the other. It was not long before he left the road and headed down to the creek. He knew every fishing hole between Millville and Barton. "Wanna come fishin with me?" He would ask every one he met on the road. The invitation was always open. He usually went alone. When the flies got too bad he would return home, but most of the time it would be near nightfall when he trudged down the grassy path to the old farmhouse. The closer he got the quicker the gait. "Mother! Look how many fish I caught today." Would be his opening statement. His mom would run her hands through his soft hair, smile and look down at him with the same kind blue eyes. She'd tell him how proud she was of his hard endeavors. One could almost see his chest swell with pride when he made this mother happy.

One morning he left earlier than usual while it was not quite dawn. He became somewhat disoriented. He was gone for a very long time and when it was becoming dusk his mom started to get a bit worried. Suddenly she heard screams coming from down the garden path. "Mother! Mother! Look what I have." He was so out of breath that he could barely talk. "Where is your shirt?" His mother asked in a laughing voice. "Here it is, mother! I got lost, and guess what I found? Look mother! My shirt is full of fiddleheads, and I have 14 trout as well. We will have a great supper tonight." His mother was bursting with pride in her son. She immediately told him to fetch me over for supper. We ate trout and fiddleheads until we were stuffed.

When Robbie grew into an ambitious teenager, he got smitten with a girl that lived down the road. I was disappointed because I knew we would have much less time together, but nonetheless I was happy for him.

All through school he was known as the jokester. Robbie made everyone laugh. His stories were delightful. After high school was completed he worked mainly in the lumber industry.

One winter it was below average in cold temperatures and Robbie was preparing for his log hauling. His co-worker told him to forget about hauling logs today, that it was far too cold. Robbie responded with, "we are hauling logs today no matter how cold it is." People could not believe what they witnessed that morning. Robbie, Charlie his helper and a team of freezing horses wrapped in blankets pushing forward in the snow with a barrel on top of the load. Robbie had the best wood stove concocted. The wood was burning brightly with orange flames shooting out of the barrel. My friend was sitting on the logs by the fire waving and smiling at every passerby. Many thought that he might be a bit touched in the head. The country boy had a plan for everything, and could always make things work out.

When his friendship with the little gal down the road took a sudden turn, I had far less time with my friend. They were together every evening. When the spring thaw came, we went off on a fishing trip together. That is when he told me that he wanted to marry Alice in the summer. "Does she know?" I asked. "No, not yet, but I plan on telling her this weekend." I responded with, "a better approach would be if you just asked her first instead of telling her, after all she does have something to say about it." We had a few chuckles over that one.

When Robbie and his bride married that summer it was an occasion that pleased all who knew them. "They were suited," as one lady put it. Forest Gump would have said, "they were like two peas in a pod." And I agree with both.

The first several years were fun years, raising their children and enjoying the community. Robbie got a job with the tax department and told one funny story after another about his tax collecting years.

I have tried to remember many of his stories. But there are so many it is hard to recall them all. I do know that it was his humor and energy that kept his lovely wife alive for many years beyond her expected journey.

One day when things were moving along fine, the children were growing into wonderful human beings, Alice got some very frightening news. She was told that she had cancer. They prayed together, knowing the dismal threat that goes along with such a dreadful disease and decided that they would leave everything in God's hands, and live life to the fullest. They laughed and loved, and did everything they could to stay positive. Alice would get her treatments without a word of complaint, and before you knew it she was well again. Fate had a life altering road for Alice. She would get another attack, and again more treatments. This went on for many years. There were sad times, but they stayed focused. They kept laughter in their hearts and home, always managing to keep their faith alive.

One hot summer day, in the early morning hours about three years ago Robbie's lovely lifetime soul mate, and true love, went on to begin her final journey. My friend was left alone. He was heartbroken, of course, but because of his humor, kindness, and energy he has been a pillar of strength to his family, community and to his church.

My friend does not have yellow hair anymore. He has never lost the energy to do whatever he sets out to do. He is a spiritual example to everyone that he meets. Now the fishing days are over and there are no more fires in barrels on top of logs to keep warm. Everyday is special to him and to those around him. He still walks with the gentle gait of a pony, and his quick smile generates a kind spirit. He has befriended many throughout his life. He has been repaid tenfold. With a birthday just around the corner, some say he is leaning toward 75. "No that can't be true. I still see the little boy in overalls goin' fishin."

Saving Martha

By Dolores Allen

Jacob was the first born of Lucy and Albert. He was a small child at birth and Lucy had a fear that he might not live. It was in the year 1906 that the child arrived and the winter came the day of Jacob's arrival. Doctors were hard to come by, and the boy was a breech birth. He was born before the Dr. could make it to the house. When he did arrive he was shocked to see such a small baby. His entire body was blue. Jacob was wrapped in warm towels to help get the blood circulating. Lucy looked down at her baby and noticed he had a dimple in his chin just like her father. She looked up at Albert and smiled saying, "isn't he beautiful?" Her husband nodded in total agreement. Albert told the neighbor that they were lucky that he was a small baby, otherwise he would never have made it. There was something different about Jacob right from the start. Neighbors starred at length when they first saw him, but they could not put a finger on what was different about this child.

Lucy and Albert lived in a three-room house that they built themselves. It was covered with cedar shingles that had turned black and weather-beaten. The well was about 300 feet from the house, and the water was carried in buckets. They heated it at the end of the stove in what they called a tank. The stove had a warming oven on the top. The house was drafty and many days due to the heavy snow, they found it difficult to get the doors open. The wash basin was kept on a wooden stand, and on very cold mornings, they would find ice floating on top. It took hours to warm the house on windy days. Layers of clothes were needed to keep out the chill. The bathroom was a wooden shack close to the house. The cracks between the boards allowed the snow to drift in. Albert put tarpaper over the boards, but the wind would rip through and tear chunks off sending it sailing through the air.

Albert was a strong man with a kindness that Lucy never took for granted. She loved him more with every passing day. She knew when she first met him that she wanted to be his wife. Albert felt the same about her. The two worked together, making a great team.

The winter was long and hard. Lucy found it difficult to tend the baby and get all the chores done. One evening there was a knock on the door and as Albert opened it, the snow came blustering in, like a frozen funnel. A young girl wearing a black cloak came floating in as if being carried by the wind. "May I come in from the cold?" She asked. Albert removed her cloak and invited her to sit by the fire to warm herself. Lucy hurried and made a pot of tea. "You must drink something hot, child. You look as though you have been out in the cold for many hours. What is your name?" The girl started to smile when she saw Jacob. She answered with, "my name is Martha, what is your baby's name?" Lucy told her that Jacob was his name. She related the details of his birth and how difficult it was. Martha listened to every word intently. "My brother looked just like him. He died at birth, but I still remember him." She continued telling Albert and Lucy that she lost her mother that day as well. "Mother never regained consciousness long enough to see her still born baby. It was a sad time for my father and I. My father, mother and I had came from Europe with very little money. The funerals were too much for him to pay. The county had to bury them. Father stayed in Canada until he could save enough money for a boat ticket home. I was left with a neighbor. He told her that he would send for me when he could arrange the money for my ticket. He never did. He became infected with a virus on the boat. They buried him at sea along with many other passengers. Some said it was from eating contaminated food. No one knows for sure. The neighbor kept me for a few months but could not continue any longer, so the county took over. I was sent to a camp to live with a couple that had a baby girl. The woman was quite ill. I was put to work immediately tending to the baby. I was only six years old at the time. I loved every minute of it though." The words seemed to run from Martha's lips, she barely stopped to breathe. "Tell us more," Lucy urged. "Well, when the baby was several months old her mother passed away. She had TB and there was no cure for her. They said it had gone too far. The man was a lumberjack, but knew little about lumbering. He was from Croatia originally, and had very little experience in the woods. The winter was brutal and the camp was freezing cold. I put the baby on the oven door to keep her warm. I was so young myself that I had to stand on a stool to stir the soup. I learned very young to make soup and peel turnips. The man's name was Eli and he had a kind heart. He barely spoke English so it was very lonely for me. I had no way to attend school. One day, when I was trying desperately to get the fire going, a knock came on the door. A man is a black suit stood in the doorway. He nearly filled the opening. I felt great fear. He began by saying in a deep voice. "What do you think you are doing child?" I replied, "I am trying to start the fire." "Don't you think you are a little too young to be playing with fire?" "The wood must be wet," I said, "or it would start to burn. The baby is cold and we have barely enough food left." I was shrieking out the words. I did not know why I was telling this stranger all of these hardships. It just came out in a flurry. The gentleman stepped aside. I could see a team of horses outside. He told me to grab my clothes and gather up the baby's things, because he was taking us to the city, where we would be looked after. He said that I would have to go to school. I began packing my clothes and a few things for the baby. In what seemed like minutes, we were out the door."

Her story continued in a somber tone saying, "that once they were seated on the sled, tears began streaming down her cheeks. Fear suddenly engulfed her entire being. What will Papa think when he comes from the woods in a few days and we are not there?" she asked the stranger. "Can't help that," he replied, "this is no place for children alone. You could freeze to death."

It was snowing and the wind was howling through the trees. Martha held the baby tight to her breast. Still weeping and feeling that she might never see Papa again was horrifying. She called Eli, papa, as she felt he was as close to being a father as she would get.

Martha learned that the stranger's name was Mr. Wilson, and that he worked for the school district checking to make sure all children were attending school. He had heard that there was a family in the woods with children that were being neglected. He did not know that Eli's wife had died. When Eli's wife, Mary, died he did not report it to the authorities, as he had no money for the burial. He put her on a sled, and told Martha to bring the baby and follow him. When they arrived at the spot that Eli had chosen to be Mary's final resting-place, he lowered his dearly beloved into the grave. He said a somber prayer. They began slowly covering the hole. He placed an "X" on a piece of wood. They silently left the wooded area and returned to the camp.

Sitting at the table that night Eli said that he would call the baby, Mary, from now on. Up to this point it had been just baby. Martha began to wonder if Mr. Wilson would question her about Mary. If he did what would she say. "Eli had told her that it was not right to bury someone without letting the authorities know. He explained to Martha that he had no other way. He had no money, and no way of getting enough to pay for a funeral."

As Martha continued telling her story the couple were shocked to learn that Martha was seven years old by then and had never set foot inside of a classroom. She was able to get her book learning when the authorities took over. They tried to get Martha and Mary cared for in the same household, but that was not to be. Martha told them that Mary screamed in terror when they pried her from her arms. She had been clinging to Martha's coat so tight that the button popped off. Tears were streaming down the young girl's cheeks as she related the sad events. Lucy and Albert sat in shock hearing the details of Martha's plight.

Martha never stopped talking, relaying details of her past experiences. They were speechless to think that this young girl had suffered so much. Martha told them that she had run away from the home where she was living because she was abused, and could not take it any longer. "Can I stay here with you for a few days? I will help take care of your baby." She begged. Lucy and Albert went into another room to discuss it. "What do you think Albert?" Lucy asked. "It's okay with me." Albert replied. "If it is all right with you. It would be a big help with the baby and the chores. You are having a hard time right now."

When they came into the living room Martha was standing by the fire holding the baby in her arms, and singing a lullaby so softly that they could barely hear her. When they told her that she was welcome to remain with them, she gave them a hug and promised that they would not be sorry. Albert was away from home a great deal of the time and she would be company for Lucy. The feed store where he worked was a couple of hours away by horse and sleigh. It made it hard for him to come home every night.

This was like a Godsend to Lucy.

Spring was just around the corner. The snow had begun to melt in patches. The sap was running in the maple trees and Lucy was eager to get them tapped to make her maple syrup. She left Martha with the child while she plodded through the snow to bore the holes. She took a kettle filled with a few slices of bread, and some cookies for her lunch. The sled was piled high carrying sap cans and spiles. She did not plan on returning until early evening. It would be a long process getting all the trees running and collecting the sap everyday. She was feeling secure having Martha in the house with her child.

Late that afternoon, Lucy began her long walk back to the house. It turned so cold that she felt as if winter had returned. The snow was still deep, and the afternoon sun made the snow softer, hence, it was much harder to walk. She kept sinking deeper and deeper until her feet were frozen. When she finally reached the house the fire was burning brightly. She sat by the bright orange and yellow flames looking at Martha and wondering how she had ever managed without her. Lucy's feet were turning color and badly in need of medical attention. Martha brought Jacob over and placed him on his mother's knee. When Lucy looked down at her child she felt a warmth go through her entire body. The color began returning in her feet and Jacob was looking at her smiling, and above his head, was a bright light. "Was it a halo?" She wondered. "Martha come here, and tell me if you see what I see?" Martha smiled, and said, "yes, I have seen this many times!" She began to tell Lucy about a day when she was alone, and cut herself very badly, and how Jacob had touched it and immediately the bleeding stopped. "I knew there was something special about Jacob from the first time I saw him. I think he has been sent by God to help many people. He has helped me forget all the bad things that happened in the earlier years. I believe he is an angel. He will be a blessing to everyone he meets. I am convinced that he is truly a gift." The two stood side by side quietly thanking God for this treasure.

The days seemed to drag by. The spring was cold. It felt like winter was still hanging on. Martha was rushing around doing the chores and Lucy was still working on the maple syrup when a horse and sleigh pulled up in front of the house. Lucy was hanging clothes on the line. They were freezing the minute they were hung. The stiff shirts came back and slapped her in the face from the brisk wind. The man on the sleigh walked over to the clothesline. "Are you Martha Dubrowski?" He asked. She answered, "yes."

"Is it true that you ran away from your boarding house some time ago?" The answer was again, "yes." "Well, I must inform you that you must return to the Browns. They have been worried sick about you. What you have done is inexcusable. They were like parents to you and you disrespected them. You have shown no appreciation for their kindness." Martha began to cry, and in a tearful voice she began to tell the man about the abuse. She explained why she ran away. The man refused to believe her. Suddenly she ran in the house and picked up Jacob. He started to cry. Lucy arrived from the sugary at that moment. The man entered the house and introduced himself to her saying that he was Fred McPhee, and was ordered to bring Martha back to the Browns. Lucy listened for a moment, and then she spoke up in a friendly voice saying. "You must not take her from here. She has had a horrific life. Being here with Jacob has saved her. Jacob has been like a healer for her. She was broken and alone when she arrived. Now she is a happy girl because of Jacob. If you take her from us he will just bring her back. He has special powers that we do not understand, but it is true." Fred looked at Jacob, and suddenly a halo appeared over his head. Fred instantly knew that he must listen to Martha and Lucy. He backed up to the doorway, then turned and left the house.

When the door closed Martha felt safe. A loud noise was heard from the path leading to the house. Running outside she found Fred lying on the ground and bleeding. "What has happened?" She asked. Fred tried to tell her how the horse broke loose, and kicked him. "I guess it was the cold." He told her. Lucy and Martha dragged him inside the house. They then sat Jacob down beside him. After a touch of the child's hand, Fred stopped bleeding and the pain was gone. "Your child does have special powers. I will do everything I can to make sure that Martha can remain with you. I can see that Jacob has given her a new life. He may have saved me too. I could have bled to death by the time I reached town. May God bless all of you." He voiced as he retreated down the path to the awaiting sleigh.

In the months that followed Mr. McPhee was a frequent visitor to Lucy's house. Many times he came with gifts, but more often he came with folks that needed healing. Jacob was a blessing to all. Martha finally found a permanent home filled with love.

Humor versus Poverty

By Dolores Allen

Gerry was driving down the highway passing every car in her path. The wind in her long red hair made her feel such a sense of freedom and excitement.

Her real name was Geraldine after her grandmother on her father's side and she resembled her grandma in almost every way. Friends began calling her Gerry on her first day of school.

As a teenager she was shorter than her peers. She carried a large bosom that did not match the rest of her profile, as did her grandma. She never knew if the boys liked her sense of humor and friendliness, or her curves. Gerry was quick with a smile and laughed at the mere hint of a joke. People said, "when she smiled she lit up the room." She could catch you off guard with her speedy wise cracks.

She came from a family that was not only lacking in material things, but all the other things that it takes to make up a happy childhood. Her grandmother was the only one who gave her encouragement. She laughed at everything her granddaughter said. Gerry would play by the hour in her gram's kitchen when she was a little girl, and wait for the hot cookies to come out of the crusty old oven. The stove was made of cast iron with a black top. It produced the best cookies and pies in the world, or so Gerry thought. The oven was used not only to bake, but also to heat the house. It was used in the spring as an incubator for the baby chickens. The fuzzy yellow birds would stagger to and fro in a box and chirp until they were old and strong enough to be put out in the coup. Gerry loved these little creatures and longed for them to remain tiny and soft, but alas, they had to grow up and become smelly hens that produced eggs for the grandparents. Later on, they would lay on a platter, legs stretched upright and golden brown to be enjoyed by the Parson for Sunday dinner when he came calling after service. Gerry would sit and stare at these birds and wonder how something so cute and cuddly could still look so appealing, with luscious smelling juices oozing out of the crisp baked skin. It seemed like only yesterday she viewed them as pets and now they were about to disappear down the Parson's gullet and make his oversized belly even larger. "Oh well, I guess it is just part of being on a farm," she would utter to herself. "Calves are cute to, but they must also be used for human consumption." One day she asked her grandmother, " why do we eat our chickens and calves? We don't eat our cats and dogs?" Grandma looked down at her and began to laugh, she did not have an answer to that, but ventured a guess, "some are farm animals and some are pets, I suppose." This answer made very little sense to Gerry, but then very little made sense to her in those days. Gerry learned early on that it did not pay to love anything too much, as it would be taken away like the fuzzy baby chicks, just to be gobbled up. She just looked for the humor in everything whether it was sad or joyful.

Gerry was a twin, but her sister died at birth, and she barely escaped the same fate. She always joked, and said that she was too stubborn to die. She did have a strong will, but her sense of humor was the ingredient that kept her going. She laughed many times when she should have cried. Her emotions ran high.

One day after Gerry's graduation from high school she was working in a community theater doing makeup for a local talent, and a voice from out of nowhere said, "you should be a comedian." She turned quickly, there stood the most vibrant looking gentleman she had ever seen. She asked, "who are you, and where did you come from?" He told her he had just arrived in town to see the show. He went on to say that he had been listening to her clowning around and assured her that she was a natural "funny girl." "This is very rare," he said. "Most talents have to be crafted and learned and practiced for years, but watching you perform and your natural ability to laugh and make your co workers laugh, was a delight to watch." With this he handed her his card and invited her to call him later that night. She chuckled out loud, "sure he wants me to call him," in a disbelieving way. With that she threw the card aside.

When several days had passed she received a phone call from this stranger, who turned out to be Bill Watson, a talent scout. He sounded excited. He almost yelled in the phone, "WOW! You were sure hard to find. I have been looking for you for a week. I have someone in a comedy club that wants to meet you. I told him about you and he wants you to come to New York as soon as possible. Will you please come?" Gerry thought for a moment and then without anymore hesitation she screamed, "YES!"

Gerry was on a plane the following Monday morning and eager to meet the challenges that lay ahead. Bill met her at the airport, and he has remained her friend, and I am happy to add that he is her life long partner. They married six months later.

She is so grateful for her poor beginnings. The baby chicks on the oven door are just one of her favorite memories, but she is thankful for all her childhood experiences that have helped to make up her comedy routine for the stage and TV.

Singing to the wind, with the top rolled down on her fancy red sports car, she is as "free as a breeze," and "happy as a lark." Yes, I know these are old clichés, but who cares. This is the exact feeling the talented successful comedian enjoys every day.

The Snow Tunnel

By Dolores Allen

Janet scurried after her brother, in and out of the clothes that were hanging on the line. Long johns and flannel shirts were frozen stiff as a board. They looked as though someone might still be in them. The wind was crisp and the sky was bright, with snow glistening like diamonds. It was a day that beckoned all the youngsters to come outside and play. Janet and her brother Theo were unaware of the events that would follow that cold wintry afternoon.

Theo heard his sister yell in an excited voice, "come and build a cave." He did not hesitate. The two children proceeded to shovel and haul snow from the side hill. Janet saw her old friend Judy approaching. "Come and help us," she called. Judy was all excited about being invited to participate in the cave digging.

The air crystallized from the cold. A cloud formed and froze in mid air with each breath the children took. Theo could hear a dog barking in the distance, but other than that there was silence.

Betty, the children's mother, was a quiet self-assured woman. She was kind and everyone liked her for her thoughtfulness. When there was sickness in the community she was the one everyone called on for help. This particular afternoon she went to help an ailing cousin.

When Janet's friend Judy came to play with Theo and Janet, Betty would invite her in for dinner. She was treated like a family member. Judy was left an orphan by the age nine. Her aunt took her in, but did not adopt her. Alice, Judy's aunt was a good caregiver, but knew nothing of child rearing, therefore, the love and affection went by the wayside. She thought that providing warm clothing and good food was all that was necessary for childcare. Many people felt the same way in those days. Give them a molasses sandwich and send them off to bed, and that would suffice all their needs. People were so busy just earning enough to put food on the table, that they had little time for anything else.

Alice was a tall stern looking woman, with silver gray hair that was pulled tight around her face and tied in a pug at the back. She wore pretty cotton dresses with a white apron over the front. She was always neat looking and almost fashionable compared to many in the surrounding area. She had pride in herself and her husband Albert was the same. He was tall and very thin. He wore V-neck sweaters and a dress shirt underneath. The collar was starched stiff and buttoned up to the neck and he donned a mustache that was waxed and trimmed ever so neatly. They never had children, although they would have been pleased to be parents, when they were younger. When folks asked why they never had a family, her answer was always the same, "we were never blessed with any." She loved her niece Judy, but did not know how to show affection. She thought that it would look silly at her age, hugging and kissing her niece, even though she may have felt like it.

Janet and Theo's father died when they were quite young. Theo thought of himself as man of the house, and he was quite proud of his role. He looked out for his mother and sister. He was very fond of Judy as well, and he treated her as an equal to his sister. Judy loved being with Janet and Theo. She would lie in bed at night and pretend that they were her brother and sister. She longed to have siblings.

Judy was a shy girl with dark brown hair that was tightly braided. Her aunt pulled it so tight that it hurt, but it did stay neat all day. The only time she felt free to be herself was when she was with her friends, Janet and Theo. Her aunt and uncle appeared to be quite stern. She felt that her aunt expected perfection.

Theo teased her relentlessly, but she did not mind. He made her laugh and they would exchange snowballs and wrestle in the snow. Life was so good for the youngsters this winter as there was plenty of snow to enjoy. There was beauty everywhere. The trio would spend hours walking through the woods following deer tracks. It was such an exciting time and they took nothing for granted. Sundays they would all sit together in Sunday school and the leisurely walk home was a time of reflection. Being young did not stop them from feeling the spiritual forces they attained from the morning sermon that followed the Sunday school. Theo loved the Pastor and helped out any time he could around the church. The Pastor's wife made molasses cookies on Saturdays. When Theo went to help tidy up the church with Pastor Don, his wife served them cookies hot out of the oven. Pastor Don teased Theo, saying he only came to help in order to sample the cookies. It was a half-truth.

The next farm was nearly a mile from Theo's house. This family was very different from others in the area. The mother rarely came out of the house except for Church and Sunday school. The father, James, possessed a superior attitude. Many said that they were too good for others in the community. Their son, Bob, was older than Theo and Janet, but he did come to play from time from time. Janet would complain to her mother that he had a cruel streak. He hurt them many times when they played. Theo would cry, when this nasty neighbor boy wrestled him to the ground, and pounded on him. The face seemed to be the main area he would aim for. One day as Theo lay in the snow after such a pounding his sister noticed the snow around him was all red. Theo was bleeding from the nose. As hard as she tried to stop the bleeding by putting snow on his forehead, and doing all that she could think of, it continued. When Betty came to his rescue, he was brought inside immediately. She tightly packed her son's nose with gauze. The packing was left overnight and by morning the bleeding had stopped. Betty felt she should speak to the parents about their son and his meanness, but declined, as she did not want to make a long-standing battle with the neighbors. One neighbor said that they had done just that, and it nearly caused world war three. "Better leave well enough alone," Betty thought.

The afternoon of digging snow and making the deep tunnel was a time of sharing. All three children talked and laughed as they took shovel after shovel full of snow out of the long passageway. Theo could barely hear the dog barking now. He was full of excitement at the depth of the tunnel and how warm it had become inside. Janet went in the house and brought out snacks. Theo placed orange crates at the far end of the tunnel. They were now very deep inside, and it was getting warmer and everything was almost silent. They could only hear the sound of their breathing and a bit of noise as they chewed on their snacks. Suddenly from the entrance of the tunnel they heard a voice yell in a nasty tone. "Come out or I will cave you in, and you will never get out." With that Theo knew it was his nasty neighbor. He started running for the exit but it was too late. The snow came falling down in heavy chunks. He began calling to Judy and Janet but there was no answer. He yelled at Bob for help, but still there was no reply. He felt he would suffocate at any moment. Fear was all he felt and the though, that his sister and their friend might never dig their way out, was horrific. Theo began to cry and pray for help. "Please God, send someone to help us."

Janet and Judy were in the far end of the tunnel and frightened beyond words. They were hugging each other tight as the snow kept falling on them. There was barely any air space now and the time would soon run out. The girls had no idea how long they had been there as they were going in and out of consciousness. "Please God, send someone to help us," they kept praying." Theo was doing the same prayer time after time. The only sound was his weak prayers, and by now he was barely breathing.

Later that afternoon down the road, Bob was sitting down at the kitchen table eating his supper when a knock came at the door. His mother, Sadie went to the door. Betty was standing in the doorway with a look of sheer terror on her face. "Have you seen Janet and Theo?" She asked. Sadie shook her head, "no" that she had not seen them. She turned to James, and asked if he had seen them that afternoon? He responded with, "no, I have not seen them since Sunday school." James was the children's Sunday school teacher. Betty was near hysterics by now. Bob sat there, not uttering a sound. He knew where the children were, but he was too much of a coward to respond.

James and Sadie brought Betty in and gave her a cup of tea, and they told her to sit by the fire until she warmed up and they would help her look for the children.

The snow was blowing so badly that there were no tracks only white drifts piled high. Betty was blaming herself saying that she should not have gone to help her cousin leaving the children alone all afternoon.

Betty was returning to her house with James and Sadie, when they saw two people walking toward them on the road. They were barely visible. It was beginning to get dark, but the wind was dying down a bit. The white outs were still blinding her vision. As the couple drew closer Betty could see that it was Alice and Albert. They looked very worried. "Have you seen Judy?" Albert asked, in a shaky voice. Betty responded with, "no, and I have not been able to find Theo or Janet. Judy is probably with them. I hope they have not wandered into the woods and got lost." James and Sadie were standing beside Betty. "Perhaps we should get all the neighbors out looking." James said.

James suddenly left them and started out on a journey to get a rescue team. Once that was accomplished he decided to stop by his house and pick up a lantern. Something seemed to tell him to go back home. Without questioning his impulse he went into his house. He found Bob sitting on a stool looking out the window and crying. "What are you crying about? I thought you didn't like Theo and Janet? By the way, do you know anything about their disappearance?" Bob began crying even harder. He was wailing now and his face was covered with fright. It was at that moment that James knew his son was responsible for their disappearance. He began to pray and ask God to forgive him for being so unkind to his neighbors when they complained about the cruel actions of his son. "Please forgive my ignorance, and please let us find the children safe." He pleaded. After his prayer he turned to his son, demanding that he tell him immediately what had happened and what he had done to the children. Bob started telling him the whole story of how he had pushed the snow in the tunnel so they could not escape. He said he was so sorry, and if he could undo it he would. Quite some time had passed, and he feared it would be too late to rescue them alive.

James began running up the road with a shovel in hand. He approached the area and barked at his son demanding that he tell him exactly where the tunnel was dug. Bob showed him where the entrance to the tunnel was, as he remembered it. Much to his surprise Bob was digging as hard as he could along side of his father. "I am so sorry," Bob kept repeating. He was repenting in a profound way. He promised his father and God that he would never do another unkind thing to his neighbors or anyone for that matter, again. James told him to just keep digging. Betty, Alice, Albert, and a few neighbors all joined in the digging. Betty noticed that Sadie was digging with her bare hands. "I will go inside and get some mittens for you," she said. Sadie was so busy she did not hear a word that Betty said, she just continued digging.

Back in the tunnel, Janet and Judy were clinging to life by keeping each other warm and twisting and turning their heads from side to side. Even this small movement was difficult as the snow was packed close to their bodies.

Closer to the tunnel exit, Theo lay with very little space. He thought if only his arms were not pressed so tightly to the wall of snow perhaps he could dig a bit and release himself, but his main fear was for his sister and Judy.

Bob's mother was still frantically digging when Betty handed her a pair of mittens. Sadie had one thing in mind and that was to save the children. She was also aware of the consequences her son Bob would face if they were not found alive. James was also very concerned. He knew that his son must be an evil child to do such a thing. He was not prepared to protect him any longer. Sadie had always protected Bob at any cost. She would even lie to James to protect him. James continued digging deeper and deeper. He wondered where his son got his mean spirit. He knew it was not from him, but maybe it could be. He never thought of his family as being anything but spiritual people. Could his son be so evil that he would have let his neighbors die? It was bad enough to do what he did, but to take so long to tell anyone where they were was almost unforgivable. James began to recall the many times he had ignored his neighbors when they needed help. He believed he did not need to do anything for anyone. He also believed that if you promised nothing then nothing would be expected of you. Now a time of reflection was upon him and he felt that God must be angry with him for being such a selfish person. His mind was racing from one thing to another. He knew Sadie was selfish, but he believed that came about because of the way she was raised. He felt her family was a lower class of people than his folks. Now, with this horrible dilemma, it was a time to reflect on his own past behavior. James did not like what he saw in himself. He whispered quietly, "no wonder Bob is so selfish and cruel." His eyes were now open and it was a sad sight to see. "How could I have been so blind for so many years?" James kept muttering over and over again.

The evening brought about calmness. The snow was lying softly on the drifts. Evenings always brought this peaceful calm at the foot of the mountain. Things were now a bit more visible as the moon was full and it shone brightly on the pure white snow. James had the lantern. Betty ran inside and brought out two flashlights, which added to the moonlight and lantern. They all continued with the task at hand. Bob was panting from his frantic digging. Everyone was beginning to get a bit weary. The pace was rapid and the energy level was dropping.

Lights were coming up the hill toward Betty's house. A full rescue team had been assembled. They were charging forward, like something from an old movie, to help. "Please let us find them alive." Betty kept whispering to herself as she dug. When the lights got closer she could tell there were many people with shovels and lights. The barking dog was running along beside the group. As he got closer, he began leaping toward the tunnel. He started digging to the left of where James was shoveling. Paws were making the snow fly in every direction. After only a few minutes of digging, he began pulling on a green scarf. "Oh my God." Betty screamed when she recognized the scarf to be that of Theo's. "Theo! Theo! Are you all right?" She screamed. She started pulling him by the collar. She noticed that he was breathing. Sobbing in his chest, she held him to her. Bob was now crying and thanking God for keeping Theo alive. The dog continued along the drift and soon he started digging again. This time it was Judy and Janet he found laying in each other's arms. When they were pulled out they were barely alive, but after being wrapped in warm blankets and a body massage they began to recover.

Judy was left at Betty's house all night and the neighbor's vigilantly watched over the children. In those days, it was difficult to get a doctor. They traveled for miles, therefore, mid wives took the place of medical teams. Betty was not a midwife, but she had become quite knowledgeable by helping the county doctor. She was sure by now the children were out of danger. Being nearly spent from exhaustion, she did not have enough energy to even feel any anger toward Bob or his parents.

James and Sadie got up early the next morning. They pulled Bob out of bed and told him to get dressed immediately. "We are going up to Betty's house and you must sincerely apologize for the dreadful thing that you have done. If you are lucky perhaps Betty will not have you arrested for the criminal act that you committed." Bob dressed in record time, and as he walked the path he told his parents how sorry he was. He said he only hoped that Betty and the children could forgive him.

Betty opened the door as soon as she saw them approaching and invited them in. "I have fresh coffee made, can I get you a cup?" She asked, Sadie nodded, "yes." "We are so sorry for what our son has done to your family, Betty, can you ever forgive us? Bob did the actual act, but we are equally responsible. We have lived a selfish life. We have been bad role models for our son. I believe he is sincerely sorry." Bob interrupted his mother by begging Betty's forgiveness. He then ran into the bedroom where the children lay on the bed.

Theo lay on his bunk bed smiling at Bob as he entered the room. Much to Bob's surprise, the girls were also smiling at him. "We are not mad at you, Bob. We believe that you are truly sorry for what you did." Theo said that he understood why Bob took so long to tell his parents what he had done. Theo assured Bob that all three of them would have a complete recovery.

As the years went by Bob and Theo bonded and became closer than most brothers. They are now sharing an apartment on campus at the same University. Bob and Janet plan to marry as soon as he is finished with his education. Betty, James and Sadie sit side by side in church every Sunday. Alice and Albert tell their daughter, every day how grateful and proud they are of her achievements, and how much they love her. Oh yes! They have adopted her. They believe she was sent to them by a higher power to fill the void in their life. Judy never leaves the house without kissing them good-bye. They are all reminded that out of every tragedy great lessons are learned. Two of the greatest is love and forgiveness. Having faith in a higher power, is of course the best lesson of all.

Mystery under the Elm

By Dolores Allen

The river was frozen with snow completely covering the ice. The crunching under foot gave an eerie sound. Mark and his pal shuffled across to the north side just in time to meet up with some friends. A stranger stood under the old elm tree that hung over the bank. "I wonder who that can be? " Mark asked his friend, but Dave failed to respond to Mark's question. "Perhaps he did not hear me," Mark thought. The old tree had been a landmark for many fisherman and hunters for decades. Some said the best fishing holes were directly under the branches that hung low nearly touching the water. In spring the water moved rapidly down river and made the most pleasant sound but now it was silent.

Mark stopped and looked at the initials that were carved in the old tree's trunk about six feet from the ground and wondered who M.J. and A.J. were? Around the initials was a heart carved deeply in the bark. "This tree must hold many secrets of many generations. It may be well over a hundred years old," Mark thought to himself.

Mark was a happy boy in his teens and could conjure up a mystery at the drop of a hat. His friends loved the intrigue that surrounded him. He was so interesting, or so his pals said. Being an only child of Avis and James Williams, he was a bit spoiled, yet he was a kind-hearted boy who was willing to share with his friends that had less than he had. He played jokes on his friends and never minded getting paid back. It was a tit-for-tat game they played. His tall stature and good looks was something that all his pals envied. Mark did not realize he was above average in looks and intelligence. His friends said he was down to earth, whatever that meant.

Mark's father, James, was not a wealthy man, but he did have more than most. He had married his childhood sweetheart Avis, and within the first year Mark was born. James inherited a paper mill that was started by his father. He quickly expanded the plant. The production tripled in a short time, and the money came pouring in. The comfort level increased immensely. James' father, John, had sent his son to a very expensive university in hopes that he would learn all there was to know about running a company. Business administration was his major. He excelled, and graduated early. He made the Dean's list, and his major was accomplished in half the time it took many of his peers. John lived only long enough to see James graduate. He died of a massive heart attack early one January morning. His son was suddenly on his own to run the mill. James spent most of his waking hours at the job site. The loss of his father and overwork began to take its toll. He grieved in silence. Avis knew how much her husband was suffering. She tried to help, but failed miserably. The gloom hung heavily over the family for many years. Mark felt the sadness in the family, and thought that it was because they were disappointed in him. He felt that he failed to inherit his father and grandfather's quick learning skills in business. That was not true, but he was sure that his father felt that way.

Both parents decided it was senseless to send Mark to the same University that James had attended. While having breakfast one morning Avis suggested that Mark might like to attend a community college where many of his friends were going. He agreed with his mother. James said it was okay with him. The next week they paid his tuition and he was enrolled in the fall semester. Mark was happy about the decision as he could remain at home while attending college, and not have to leave his friends.

The young man had a loving relationship with his mother. Avis would talk for hours about her childhood and repeatedly relay stories about her father and mother who had passed away when she was a very young girl. She told Mark that she never wanted her father and mother's memory to die, and by repeating the stories to him, it would keep their spirits alive. She was adamant about this. Many pictures of her father and mother were shown regularly to her son. Each time the pictures were viewed; he noticed a photo of a gentleman that looked similar to his grandfather. The man had the same style of clothes. When Mark questioned his mother about the man she would just mutter, "oh it is just an old friend of your grandmother." It looked to Mark, as though they might have been from a foreign country. One photo showed her father sitting beside, what his mother described as an old wash tub. The surrounding grounds were unkept, and the gardens were over run with weeds. "Where was he sitting?" he asked his mother. She replied, "he was at his mother's house." "But mother, they look so poor, were they that poor?" Avis did not answer; she turned and walked down the path to the house with her head hung low. Mark knew that this must be a sore spot with her. "I must not ask these questions again," he thought.

Mark kept looking at the man standing under the tree and wondering who he could be. Why was he remembering the stories so vividly now that his mother had told him about her father and mother? "Oh yes," he thought, "it is because he is wearing the same kind of hat that they wore." Mark had seen many pictures of his grandfather and he was always wearing the same hat. "But why is this man watching me so closely?" Mark wondered. When Mark got closer he became engrossed in talking with his pal and forgot about the man in the strange hat. When he arrived at the tree there was no one there. "Where did that man go?" He asked Dave. "What man?" His friend asked. "I didn't see anyone there." "But he was standing there all the while we were walking toward the tree. You must have seen him, I did." Mark said in an almost begging voice. Both boys decided to drop the subject and go on with what they were doing.

Summer went by swiftly and fall was closing in. It was an exciting time for all the boys. They hustled about getting new clothes and books for college. Mark was not sure which subjects to sign up for in the first semester. He decided to consult a school counselor for advice. After much thought and some coaching from the counselor and his father he decided to study accounting. It would have been better at the University, but this was next best his mother said. He went into his classes with a passion. He studied hard being determined to make his parents proud. Dave was in the same class, and he worked equally as hard. When the Christmas papers were handed in they both felt confident that they had done extremely well. They were right, Mark was second in his class and Dave came in first.

With both boys finishing their first semester of college, and now reaching the age of eighteen they were feeling quite grown up, even a bit macho. Girls were beginning to notice them and somehow their thoughts were drifting in

111

that direction as well. A few days of ice fishing and a bit of skiing, that was what they had all been waiting for. Dave said in a laughing way, "I hear there are lots of cute girls on Crabbe Mountain around the Christmas holidays." Mark answered, "ya, so what?" Both boys trotted off laughing.

The first day of vacation was set aside for ice fishing. Several of Mark's pals gathered together for a day of cutting ice and frying fresh trout. Mark brought the frying pan and Dave hauled the wood to make the fire. Several of the boys brought fishing gear and snacks. Snow had gathered deep on the river. Mark began wading ahead of his mates heading straight for the big elm tree. He could not believe what he saw. There was the same old man standing under the tree wearing the same clothes. He wondered why he appeared there on such a cold windy day. December was always cold and snowy in that particular area. Mark yelled at Dave over the wind, "look! There is that same stranger that was here before, do you see him now?" When Mark turned away from Dave, he looked toward the elm tree and there was no one there. "Where did he go in such a hurry?" Mark wondered. Dave was yelling back, "I don't see anyone." "Never mind," Mark said, "He is gone. Hurry up and build the fire."

Mark and Dave began to pick at the ice. It was not long before the hole was big enough, and they started angling. The other young men had picked away until they had their holes dug as well. Mark kept looking at the elm tree, waiting to see the stranger, but he did not return that afternoon. The boys kept pulling trout out of the holes. The fish had round bellies, and when they were cleaned they were still fleshy, and "oh sooo sweet tasting." "Fried in butter is the only way to go," Mark said. Dave prided himself in cooking trout. He claimed to be the best in the county. Mark thought he was, but he gave Dave the honors.

Darkness was approaching and the boys decided to pick up their gear and head for home. "How about going skiing tonight?" Dave shouted above the wind. "Good idea," Mark answered. All the boys were in accord.

That evening the boys raced up and down the mountain competing with one another. Who could go the fastest was the main thing on their agenda. Mark was racing down the hill, and to his left, standing by the fence he noticed a young girl hanging on the rail. She appeared to be crying. "What is wrong?" Mark yelled to her as he veered left and into her path with snow flying. "Are you okay?" He asked in a softer voice now that he was closer. She told him that her name was Amy. Mark responded by telling her that she had a pretty name. "I am named for my grandmother," she said. "Amy Jones was my grandmother. She died a few years ago. Today is the anniversary of her death. I have been very sad today. I thought perhaps if I came skiing I might feel better, but the sadness has stayed with me. You go on, and continue skiing with your friends. I am okay. Just a wee bit down today. Thank you anyway for caring." "Do you feel like talking about it?" He asked. The story began to unfold as Amy told him how her grandfather took her grandmother ice fishing by the old elm tree. "It was a very mild day just before Christmas. Grandfather was standing by the old tree carving their initials in the bark when the ice gave way. As hard as grandfather tried to save her, it was hopeless." Amy continued on by telling Mark how her grandfather stood under the tree every day after his wife died talking to her as thought she were still there. He died a few months later. Mark stood listening with tears in his eyes. "Amy, I don't know how to tell you this, but your grandfather is still there. I have seen him two times already. He disappears every time I get close. No one else seems to see him, but I do. Come with me tomorrow morning and I will show you. Meet me at eight on the riverbank, and we will cross the river to the tree together. You will see him. I know you will be able to see him, as I do."

The evening wore on and the air commenced to warm up. Mark and Amy spent the rest of the evening together. His pals began teasing him about his new girl friend, but Mark just laughed. When it was time to leave, Mark made Amy promise to meet him in the morning.

Mark had a restless sleep. He kept thinking about the stranger under the tree. "What if he does not appear? I will look silly. Amy will think it was just a ploy to gain her interest." Going in and out of dreams of the river, and overflowing banks, he could feel the cold water rising up his legs unto his torso, and over his head; then trying to save Amy from the rushing water. Dreams of running the paper mill and failing. So many mixed up dreams, school failure, Amy. Disappointing his parents was one of his worst nightmares. The old man by the tree seemed to be somewhere in all of his confused dreams. After several hours of having these horrendous dreams, he decided to get up and watch television. He could hardly wait for morning. He realized that one reason for his restlessness was the anticipation of seeing Amy again. He had just met her, but he knew that she was a girl he wanted to get to know a lot better. He sat watching the clock and when the time arrived he took a quick shower, and then bolted out the door, and down to the riverbank.

Amy held out her hand to him. He rushed to her side. Before he realized what he was doing he gave her a big bear hug. Hand in hand they strolled across the river. They talked endlessly about everything. Suddenly Mark looked up, and there under the elm tree stood the stranger. "Amy do you see him?" He whispered. "Yes, oh Mark it is my grandfather. He is waiting for us." The two youngsters began running toward him. Suddenly the ice gave way, then a powerful force took over their bodies pulling them to shore. "Grandfather you have saved our lives!" Amy shouted. Grandfather stood there smiling, and with a wave of his hand he bade them, goodbye "Amy, I thought that perhaps the stranger was my grandfather, but he is yours. God has sent your grandfather to put us together." Mark said. He began to pull the pictures of his grandparents from his pocket. There was also a picture of his grandmother's friend. Amy stared at the picture, knowing that she must tell Mark the truth, as she knew it. "Mark, the man in the picture is my grandfather. He was in love with your grandmother a long time ago. His parents would not allow them to marry. Your grandmother had a child sired by my grandfather, but he died when he was two years old. Your grandmother suffered great hardship until she married your grandfather, John." Mark responded quickly "Yes, I believe every word, but why did my mother never tell me this part of the past? She told me so many stories about my grandparents, but never this," Mark was in utter confusion. Amy began telling Mark what she knew, beginning in a solemn voice. "There was a part of the past that no one ever talked about, and that was your grandmother. Perhaps your mother never revealed any of this to you because she was ashamed of her mother's past. After grandfather married my grandmother they moved away. It was on a return visit for a Christmas holiday with relatives that the accident happened. Even after he passed away, many folks said he returned daily. You were not the only one to see grandfather standing under the tree. Other members of our family have witnessed the same vision."

Amy leaned forward and hugged the tree. "Thank you grandfather," she whispered, "for sending Mark to me, and for pulling us to the shore before we were swept away like grandmother."

Mark and Amy walked the river many times in the years to follow, but they never saw grandfather again. Amy said that, he must have finally gone to rest with grandmother.

Mark never let his parents down. His mother was a private woman. Therefore he decided that she did not need to know that he had discovered the family secret.

The young couple quickly became soul mates and married the following spring. They thanked the old man under the tree for putting them together. They knew it was God's plan. Folks around said that it was meant to be.

Dave and Mark have remained best friends. Dave became plant manager and is now part owner of the mill.

Under the initials on the old elm tree there lies another set of initials carved inside of a huge heart. The bark is hued to perfection and reads "A.J. loves M.W." Under the heart there is a message. "Thank you grandfather."

The Gift

By Dolores Allen

Life in the country was hard for Sara and Jeff. Betty, the children's mother would yell, "bring in the wood, get the water." She fell into a pattern of feeling sorry for herself when her husband died. Many times she took her anger and disappointments out on her son and daughter. She was not an appreciative woman, but she did have respect for her children and for their efforts to make her life easier. She knew that without them life would have no meaning whatsoever. She was proud of their kind spirit, and how they loved a challenge.

Early spring was an exciting time for the children as they spent most of their time trying to earn a bit of spending money by cleaning up yards for the neighbors.

Jeff got a brain wave one day, and said to Sara, "what do you say we get a hen and some eggs and hatch some baby chickens to sell? We could get them from gram. Perhaps we could take them to market." Sara was so excited, she screamed. "We could even have our own eggs then mother would not be able to stop us from eating all the eggs we wanted. It is so exciting, Jeff. Can we go ask grandmother now?" Off the two ran through the tall wet grass to gram's house. Before nightfall they had arranged for the eggs and a borrowed hen to sit on the eggs.

Weeks went by and everyday Jeff and Sara would check the eggs. A few days before the chickens were to hatch there was a horrendous thunderstorm.

Betty began to worry. She told the children that loud thunder could harm unhatched eggs. It did not take long for the pair to realize their mother's fear was well founded. When it had gone past the due date for the chicks to hatch, it did not happen. They opened the eggs and one by one they discovered there was a baby chick in each egg, but all were dead from the storm. The brother and sister stood holding hands and cried for the loss of their baby chicks.

The summer passed quickly and it was time for them to return to school. Just a few short weeks later they woke up to find the hills and the paths covered by the first snowfall. The fluffy white powder glistened like white diamonds. The crackling sound when they stepped outside was like magic. Both children loved the winter and the excitement of the first snow was thrilling. This magical time was a prelude to Christmas. Excitement was building, but the children were very worried as they had little money saved to buy Christmas gifts.

Their mother was widowed at a young age and left with no money, therefore making it difficult for her to buy presents for the children. The children were determined to make it up to her. "We must earn money for Christmas somehow," Jeff said to Sara. "Oh and don't forget presents for gram," Sara spouted, "gram will want yarn to make more socks, don't you think?" "But how are we going to get enough money for that many gifts?" Jeff whined. Sara had a great scheme in the back of her mind. "I heard that there was a man that came through the settlement buying bottles, fur hides, and rabbits. Maybe we could get traps to catch some animals to sell." Jeff quickly responded with, "do you think anyone around here would have any old traps that they would let us use?" "Well," Sara said, "I know that Uncle Pete had traps and he does not go trapping anymore, want me to ask him?" "Yes," replied Jeff.

Sara was not long coming home with a box full of old traps and wire to make snares. With much excitement, she screamed, "Uncle Pete will buy anything we catch, but we must start right away. We don't have that much time before Christmas."

Early Saturday morning the two children trudged through the deep snow toward the woods. They saw rabbit tracks everywhere. The boughs on the spruce trees were trimmed with glistening white snow and the soft winter breeze made them hang low, and wave as if in a friendly gesture. The quiet was deafening. Soon they reached Stony Brook. The stream was partly frozen over, but the crystal clear water was still running in swirling patterns down the rocky bed. Beauty was everywhere, and the two children were in tune with the greatness of what nature had provided for them. Jeff said, "let's just sit on this log and look around and remember all the scenery as we now have it, and let us never forget this moment." Sara whispered, as she did not want to break the quiet, "I will always remember this moment, I promise."

By the first day the young trappers had set 10 traps and 15 snares and now all they had to do was visit them every day to collect their catch. Day number one was very discouraging. The catch was one rabbit. "This is not going to bring much money for us." Sara said, "Don't worry it will get better, Sara." Jeff reassured her. Please do not get discouraged, as I need you to help me tend the traps" "It's okay Jeff, I won't let you down." Sara answered in a consoling voice.

On the third day the children were elated. They arrived home with their catch, shouting, "Mother! Look what we caught." They stood holding three rabbits and a little white ermine. "What a happy day this has been," said Sara, smiling at her mother. "We will go to Uncle Pete's house right away and see how much he will pay us."

Betty watched as her children returned from their uncles. They were walking down the garden path still carrying their catch and looking very sad. Upon entering the house Sara began crying and in an angry voice spouted, "uncle just said he would buy our catch, he did not mean it, he just laughed. He said, there have been no buyers for these animals for years. I was playing a joke on you."

A week went by before the children felt like tending their traps and snares again. They knew they might as well bring them in and return them to their uncle, but the joy they felt when they placed them now eluded them, as they sadly walked the paths to collect them. Jeff looked at Sara with tears in his eyes and said. "Sara it is so awful to be poor! I want so much to buy nice presents for you and mother and gram, but I don't see how I am going to do it if we can't sell the furs. Uncle has a mean spirit and he hurt me. I shall never forgive him." "It's okay," Sara said with a smile, "I do not need any presents anyway. I was going to buy uncle a warm scarf, but now I don't think I will buy him anything, even if I have the money." Jeff looked away from Sara, and the solace he felt here in the densely wooded forest gave him a sense of place. He knew he could not stay angry with Uncle Pete.

"Sara," Jeff was speaking very softly, "lets not stay mad at Uncle Pete, he was just playing a joke on us. I think he meant no harm, okay?" Sara was in agreement and they started for home. A loud scream came from Sara's mouth and she began to stutter. "What is it Sara?" Jeff asked. "Look over here! I don't know what it is, but it is sure bright and different than anything I have ever seen before. It is very heavy Jeff, can you help me carry it?" The children left the traps and snares and walked up the hill toward the house. They placed the foreign object in the shed and locked the door for safekeeping.

Jeff was running to the mailbox when he noticed his uncle walking toward him. Uncle Pete was smiling. He began with a kind voice saying, "Jeff, I am sorry that I played a joke on you. I have been calling many places, and I think I may have a place to sell your furs" This made Jeff feel much better. He quickly thanked him and proceeded to tell him about the foreign object that Sara had found. They went inside the shed to look at the piece of metal that Jeff was talking about. His uncle was astonished to see such a piece of foreign material. He told the children that he was almost sure it was a meteorite. "We will take it to the University at once and have them tell us what it is." Sara and Jeff could not wait for the news. Sara almost screamed, "perhaps we have contributed something very important to science. They may even put a plaque on the wall with our names on it for just finding it." "Oh Sara, you have such a wild imagination." Her brother retorted.

Christmas was coming fast. Jeff and Sara still had no money for presents. They had heard nothing from the University. Uncle Pete told them he was waiting to get a fair market price for the furs so there was no money forthcoming. The children were becoming very discouraged and the excitement of getting the tree up and trimmed had little meaning these days. Jeff said, "what good is a tree without presents?"

Later that afternoon they saw their gram hurrying up the path with a basket in her hand, which held a huge chicken and a Christmas pudding. The children were happy about the gifts, but sad too, as they had no presents for her. Walking, holding gram's hand, they heard a car coming up behind them. Suddenly two large gentlemen got out and walked toward them. The pair bewildered Jeff. Both men were wearing heavy coats and high boots. They sported heavy beards and on their heads sat tall black hats with stiff brims that might have been something like a gangster would wear. When the older man spoke it was with an accent. He began by asking if they knew a

Jeff and Sara Wilson. Jeff said, "that's me!" Without hesitation the stranger said, "I am professor Eisenbiser and this is my son, Eric. We are from the University. They have authorized me to make an offer of purchase for the meteorite you sent us. I have a check for $5,000, if you are interested. I know you will have to get permission from your parents to make this decision." Without hesitation the children ran up the hill screaming, "Mother! Mother! Come outside now, we have good news." Betty came outside and in a sad note told them there was no such thing as good news. She was full of grief most of the time, but even more so around this time of year. "But mother," Jeff cried, "it is good news, please come with us and we will show you." Betty was standing in the doorway with her hand over one eye to block out the sun, and in a nasty voice wailed, "who are those two men down there with your grandmother?" "That is what we are trying to tell you, mother. They are from the University and they want to buy our meteorite for $5,000. Will you give us permission to sell it?"

Betty, after some hesitation ushered the two gentlemen in and seated them at the kitchen table. The elderly gentleman placed many papers on the table for Betty to examine. They suggested that should she have any concerns, to feel free to contact an attorney and perhaps he could make things clear for her. Betty learned that Eric was about her age and had become widowed about the same time as she. The hours began to drag on as they talked about many personal things. By the time the business was concluded and the papers were signed they had become fast friends.

Jeff and Sara were now in a joyful mood. They began laughing and chattering about Christmas gifts for everyone. Suddenly they stopped, and in a joking way they asked the pair if they would join them for Christmas dinner. Jeff suddenly looked very sad, and followed with, "there have been many lonely Christmas' since daddy died and it would be nice if you could share the day with us. Mother would like it, I am sure. Would you like it mother?" The professor declined the invitation, saying he would be in Europe over the holidays due to an ailing sister, but Eric said he would be delighted. As they were leaving, Eric turned and gave Betty and the children a big hug. He smiled when he got past the door and said, "I have had many lonely Christmas' too. I will see all of you Christmas day?" Oh, by the way, what about New Years? With a happy giggle Betty responded, "and how about every Sunday?

God's Special Treasure

By Dolores Allen

Lying in the carriage on the front porch, Natalie lay kicking and screaming for attention. She had a brother and a sister a few years older. Natalie's brother Albert, was a tall lanky boy with hair cropped short and an attitude. He was smarter than most people, or so he thought. He mocked and jeered everyone, thinking that was humor, regardless of how hurtful. He made fun of his parent's and sisters. Albert constantly corrected everyone. The parent's of the three were especially proud of their son. Everything he said and did was funny in their mind. They were totally unaware that he had a sadistic personality. The older sister Bea, was a bit slow and, cried at the drop of a hat. She was not mentally challenged, just borderline. She had a chubby face and short fat legs that rubbed together when she ran. Under her chin was a huge dark birthmark. Her dark blond hair was straight and parted in the middle. She had many features of a Down's Syndrome child, however they were not predominate. The kids in the neighborhood said that she looked like a cartoon character. Natalie on the other hand had short dark hair with a natural wave. She learned in her carriage that crying got her what she wanted. Her brother detested her because of her constant whining and her spoiled demeanor. She was unaware of his feelings. She adored him and saw him as a hero. Whatever he said she believed it to be gospel.

Being the youngest she felt she should have the best. Her older sister and brother were just put on the earth to be her servant and supply all her needs.

Her brother got tired of catering to her and began to rebel. Natalie, in her whinny voice would say, "I don't feel good." That was all she needed to say and her mother, Wendy, would shift all the responsibility to Bea and Albert. She would lay about not wanting to get ready for school, thus making her brother and older sister wait for her. Each morning it became harder to get her dressed and out the door. Her older siblings were feeling more and more disgust.

Bea was a girl with a quick temper. Her parents would say, "give it to her so she won't get angry." The girl had no patience and hated anyone or anything that was different. She despised people that were slow, and her intolerance got worse with each passing year. She would lie on the floor kicking and screaming until she passed out, if her parents denied her anything. This continued until school age. It became a control mechanism, knowing that having a temper tantrum would get her everything.

Christmas was a nightmare for the parents. What to buy, how to make sure they were of equal value, was a worry. The tears would begin abruptly if the presents were not to their liking. Wendy and her husband Allen dreaded Christmas.

Friends became scarce. The relatives developed a dislike for the family because of the children's bad behavior. They began to stay away. Wendy, Allen, and the three children sat alone a great deal of the time. The neighbors' children did not want to play with them.

One bright sunny spring morning the next door neighbor Judy, came home from hospital with a new baby boy. She was a first time mom and very excited about her baby. Judy loved being home with her son. Her husband had a great job that provided nicely. This allowed Judy to remain at home to raise her baby. Judy was a spiritual woman. She would thank God everyday for the wonderful son he had given her and for her husband Frank. The little guy was a happy child and smiled at everyone that came near him. The baby was named Peter, after the Apostle. When he was only two weeks old, his parents began taking him to Church and Sunday School. He would lay in his carriage and never make a fuss. When Peter was about one year old, his mother noticed that there was something different about her son. He did not seem to progress as quickly as many children his age. When other one-year-old babies were walking and creeping, Peter was scooting across the floor on his bottom. Legs outstretched he pulled himself in a quick motion. He would pull his legs in and with the grace of a ballerina, hustle from one side of the room to the other, laughing all the while. It was a wonderful sight to watch him in motion. His mom began reading many books on children with learning disabilities. One day she picked up a religious magazine. Lo and behold there was a picture on the cover of a boy that looked much like her son. The headline jumped off the cover at her. It said, "God's Special Treasure." She always knew there was something special about her baby, now she was sure. He was indeed a gift from above. She began to read about a test that could be done while the mother was carrying the child to detect if the child would be deformed or have Down's Syndrome. Many women were having the test done, and if there was any chance of either, they could have the child aborted. Peter's mother began to weep as she stared at her son, and then at the picture of the baby on the cover. "How could anyone even think of aborting such a lovable child?" She wept.

As Peter grew older his good spirit grew by leaps and bounds. He smiled at everyone and hugged anyone who would stand still. Those, that allowed God's special treasure to come into their lives, were truly blessed. The ones that rejected him did not do it to be mean spirited, they failed to understand the situation. By rejecting God's little son they were unknowingly rejecting one of God's masterpieces. He came here to teach us tolerance and love and those that accepted him enjoyed the pleasure of his kindness.

Bea especially disliked Peter. Natalie was tolerant of him, because she did not want anyone to know how she really felt. Albert had absolutely no time for him. He would shout, "get out of my yard." Peter would walk away with his head down not knowing what he did to cause this outrage.

"God did not make us all perfect," someone once said. Many of us believe that in God's eyes "we are ALL perfect." As Peter grew older he attended church every time there was a service. He smiled and hugged all the parishioners. The spirit he emitted was overwhelming. Many of the church attendants were amazed at how much joy he brought to the elderly who sat alone day after day. If it had not been for the visits from Peter, they may not have received any company at all.

Back to the spoiled children next door, things remained the same. They now had someone that they could mock. They were absolutely cruel to Peter. Their mother, Wendy would say grace at the dinner table, but the rest of the mealtime was used up making fun of Peter. The sweet little boy was the brunt of most of their jokes. When they got tired of making fun of him they always found some other poor unsuspecting soul to criticize and ridicule.

Mrs. Brown, the neighbor on the opposite side of Peter was not religious, but she was a spiritual woman. Everything she did and said was kind and thoughtful. When Peter came to visit, she greeted him with open arms. She tried to give back the love that he showered on her. Her grandmother taught her, as a little girl, that every time you hurt one of God's children, you made Jesus cry. That stuck with her on into adulthood. One day when Peter was leaving his neighbor's house to go home, he stopped and faced the door for a moment. Then turning around, he looked directly into Mrs. Brown's eyes, and asked in a stumbling voice, "will you come to church with me tomorrow?" Mrs. Brown could see tears in his eyes. She said with a smile, "of course Peter, I would love to come to church with you."

Sunday morning, Peter arrived at Mrs. Brown's door to collect her. The neighbor was ready. Arm in arm they walked to the nearby church. Peter sat with his arm around Mrs. Brown all during service. The woman felt as though the spirit of God was touching her soul. She knew she was receiving a love that only the Supreme Being could emit. It was being sent through this little mentally challenged boy. It was as though Christ was sitting beside her. She knew she was definitely in His presence. A change was coming over her and her emotions were bringing her to tears. She began to pray and thank God for sending Peter to her. Most of the congregation gave thanks for this child of God, who had taught them so much. Mrs. Brown called him a treasure and thanked him for bringing her to such a peaceful place. She was now a child of the almighty God.

Not everyone felt the same in the service. There was one exception, and that was the neighbors on the other side. They sat there without uttering a word. In their mind he was anything but a treasure. He was a nuisance.

When the spoiled three-some reached home and were seated around the fancy dining room table, Albert said, "what was that all about this morning? What was Mrs. Brown trying to prove? Is she losing it or what? How can she sit there hugging a retarded boy like that?" Natalie responded with, "She was just making a show for herself." Bea looked angry and blurted out, "I can't stand those kind of people. He gives me the creeps when he comes near me."

When the weekend was over, Bea set out to go fishing. It was against their religion to fish on Sunday, therefore she had to wait until Monday. The river was full and flowing rapidly from all the rain. The fish had many deep holes to hide. "A great fishing day," Bea thought, as she trudged through the brush to reach the stream. The smells from the damp moss, and the cedar trees were like perfume to Bea. She was ecstatic, as fishing was one of her passions. Bea arrived home around noon and proudly showed the trout to her Mom. She was on her way back to the river again when she noticed Peter pick up an apple from the ground in their orchard. "Put that apple down! You little thief. Don't you ever steal another apple from this orchard or I will do something drastic to you." Without hesitation Peter said, "I am sorry I made you angry, and I won't eat your apples again." Bea shouted back. "What are you saying. All I hear is mumbling. I can't understand a word that you say. Just stay away from here." The young lad walked away with his head hanging down carrying a sorrowful look. Bea did not know that the boy was praying for her. He was whispering, "please God don't be mad at Bea. She did not mean to be angry with me, she was just protecting her mother's apples. Forgive me Father for stealing." Not one person could have understood his prayer, but I am sure God understood every word.

Over on the other side of the river, Bea saw a deep fishing hole. Eagerly she jumped on a log to cross the river at the narrowest point. Upon arriving midway her foot slipped on some soggy weeds that the log had caught as they floated down river. She lunged forward and fell into the stream. The water was reaching her waist and she was screaming for help. It was ice cold spring water rushing with great urgency. Knowing that the water deepened very quickly, she knew she was in trouble. The water was swirling around her waist. Then it began creeping up to her chest and pulling her back and forth. She began to panic. Her heart was pumping fast and her screams were getting louder. Her brother could hear her all the way from the house. He was so attuned to her screaming about everything that he ignored the cries for help. As far as he was concerned she could drown. He did not seem to care in the least. Under his breath he chuckled and chanted. "Let her drown."

When Natalie came out side and heard her sister's screams she suggested Albert go to see if she was in trouble. He just laughed, "oh she is just crying wolf again. You know how she is." He jeered. Bea could not understand why some of her family was not coming to her rescue. She knew that they could hear her. It was not that far away. She was shouting loud enough. "Please someone help me," she cried, as she began to slip further away from the log. Suddenly Bea could hear a noise in the distance like someone running on the branches that had collected on the path. Whoever it was, she knew they were moving swiftly. She heard a stammering voice saying, "I'm coming. I will help you. I'm coming, I will save you Bea." She soon realized it was Peter. For the first time she could understand his halting voice. "Oh no, what can he do?" She thought. Peter came running with a long pole in his hand. Reaching the pole out to Bea he began pulling her out of the water. Bea could not believe how strong he was. "How could a little retarded boy do this?" she thought. When she looked into his eyes she saw a light that shone right through her and her heart began racing. She felt the presence of God. He had sent Peter to rescue her. Bea knew that Peter did not do this on his own. When she returned home and told them of the experience and how Peter had saved her life, her brother laughed. He did not believe a word. Her mother told her to go and get dry clothes. When Bea was finished, her father and mother spoke to all three children. "Tonight we will have a family meeting and you will all listen to what we have to say. We have much to talk about."

When the time arrived, Albert, Natalie and Bea all sat in a row, wondering what was going to happen. Their father Allen was patient and a man of few words, but when he did speak it meant something. Wendy was more like the children and did not hesitate to mock people along with her son and two daughters. Allen began, "I have been talking to the pastor and many neighbors about your behavior and apparently they all believe that all three of you are badly in need of an attitude adjustment. Your mother has not been much help in this area. She has let you mock neighbors and hurt people and, most of all, hurt each other. I have ignored all of these things, saying I was too busy, but now it is time I take charge. I can no longer ignore the situation. I only hope it is not too late. Bea, you could have died today and your brother and sister did not lift a finger to help. The boy next door, that you have mocked for years, saved your life. He has more spirit and heart than all three of you put together. He has brought Mrs. Brown to God and he has saved your sister's life. Who is the superior one? Albert we know it is not you. Natalie, Bea, and you are incorrigible. The young lad next door is a blessing to all. You three are snobs and think of no one but yourselves. I have a feeling that you only pray for yourself, if you pray at all. From this day forward, Peter will be welcome in our home. He will be revered as a special child. If you cannot accept this, then perhaps you will have to spend many hours in your room because Peter will be at our dinner table whenever he chooses. You have many fences to mend, then and only then, will I start to respect you. You must ask God for forgiveness if you expect to be a part of this family and a part of the human race. Right now you three have separated yourselves from the rest of the community. Because of your arrogance you stand-alone and will remain that way if you do not make a change. Try to learn something from Peter." Bea spoke up quickly, "I have already learned from Peter. I believe he had a special power that helped him pull me out of the river. He is so much smarter than I thought. I am so grateful that he saved my life. I will make it up to him. I will never tell him to stay away from me again, or chase him from the orchard." Albert and Natalie were sitting in silence and feeling a bit ashamed. They immediately excused themselves and went upstairs to bed.

It was daybreak when Albert and Natalie woke up. They both had a restless night. Albert started to say his prayers and before he knew what was happening a rush of warmth entered his body. He immediately fell asleep and began to dream. He was floating on a pink cloud and Peter was pulling him and laughing. The mumbling began, but instantly Albert could understand every word he was saying. In the next room, Natalie was having the identical dream.

Suddenly startled by their father's voice coming up the stairs they jumped from their beds and hurried down to the dining room. Natalie began helping her mother in the kitchen, which she never did before. Albert sprang to his feet and started setting the dining room table. He looked at his father with a tear in his eye and said. "You will hear no more jokes or nasty comments from me around the dining room table. I had a dream last night that made me feel even more ashamed than I did last night. Father, I am sorry that I have been so insensitive to you and everyone." Natalie began to cry. She said, "I am so sorry for being such a selfish sister." Albert reached out and put his arms around both sisters and said, "Natalie, Bea and I are sorry for being so unkind to you and for being so uncaring. I will try to change. Peter has taught us all a lesson."

Christmas morning was a joyful time at Wendy's house for the first time. Peter arrived and quickly knocked on their door early in the morning mumbling words Wendy did not understand. He handed her a basket filled with homemade jelly and jams that he had helped his mother make. "Where is Albert?" He asked, in a sorrowful voice, hoping that he had not gone away for the holidays. Albert ran out of the kitchen toward Peter and hugged him around the neck. He dragged him into the living room where the Christmas tree was lit up. "Here are your presents," chanted Natalie and Bea. Peter mumbled in a tearful voice, "I only have presents for your mother. I have nothing for you. I cannot accept these gifts if I have nothing for you in return." Albert turned facing Peter. He placed his hands on the boy's round cold cheeks and looked into his sad eyes. With a tearful smile, he said in a pleading voice, "Peter will you be our brother? If you will, that will be our Christmas gift." Peter laughed and muttered the answer in an incoherent voice, but the children understood every word. Wendy and Allen stood in the doorway giving thanks to God for allowing them the best Christmas ever. With bowed heads. They all said. "Amen."

The Reunion

By Dolores Allen

Karen stood by her computer trying to decide whether to go online and make reservation or forget the entire thing. Suddenly her fingers drifted up and down the keyboard. Before she knew it, she saw the flag in the corner of the screen saying you have mail. With great urgency, she clicked on the mailbox, and there it was in black and white. "You have your ticket, do you wish to have it mailed or would you like it sent via e-mail? Your itinerary will follow in a few hours. You will be flying Delta from the Metropolitan airport.

Gazing at the screen, she wondered if she had done the right thing. Being sad for so long, she wondered if she would be in any frame of mind to go to this reunion. She felt she must always look happy and never show anyone how she really felt. Karen learned how to hide sadness at an early age. Never let anyone know how you really feel, that had become her motto.

Consumed with work, and trying to make a success of her life, did bring some peace and contentment for many years. She had a son that gave her great joy. Karen was proud of Tom. He was an achiever. No challenge was too great for this young man, be it sports or scholastics. When Karen handed him the keys to a new red sports car for his graduation, he could not wait to try it out and show it to his girlfriend. He raced out the door and drove directly to Sue's house with his shiny masterpiece.

It was on a foggy night that Tom left the house to take Sue to the prom.

131

He looked like a picture on the cover of a magazine, Karen thought. She kissed her son goodbye and wished him a good night. "Drive carefully, as it is quite foggy and very difficult to see." She told him. Karen stood and proudly watched as her son hurried down the sidewalk

Now she was sitting in a hospital waiting room for what seemed like an eternity. A tall gentleman approached Karen and asked if she was Tom's mother and of course she smiled and said, "yes." "I'm Dr. Anderson, I just finished operating on your son. The head injury was impossible to repair. It is with great sadness that I have to tell you this, but your son did not make it through surgery. I have tried to get in touch with your family physician, but I have been unable to reach him. I will continue to try, and as soon as I do, he will call you with all the details." "Are you all right, Mrs. Jones?" The Doctor asked in a concerned manner. Karen smiled her self-assured smile and said she was quite all right. She would not cry for fear she might never stop. All feelings were buried deeply. She never allowed herself the privilege of letting go. "Hang on Karen," she said to herself as she stumbled out the revolving door of the emergency entrance. "Don't let anyone see you cry."

In another city, several hundred miles away, a drama was being played out in another fashion. Only this drama did not have the same ending. Kevin was sitting at his kitchen table holding a letter in his hand from his only son, Tim. Staring at the letter and reading it over and over again, it still made no sense. "Dad, I love you, but I will not return. It has nothing to do with you. It is not your fault but! but! but!" So why did he choose to do this if it had nothing to do with me? The father asked himself? Time after time Kevin read and reread the letter. The tears were flowing freely. Kevin wondered, "how could he just leave without talking to me first?" He began to write a letter, in response to his son, with many questions. He begged for a meeting to talk things over. It took a few days of trying to find an address. He finally found an address of one of Tim's old friends. He was sure this friend would know how to get in touch with his son. As the days, weeks and months went by, and there was no reply to his letter, he feared the worst.

Kevin, much like Karen, plunged into work as a solace. Hard work and long hours helped deaden the pain of losing Tim. Kevin began to understand why Tim had left, but he was unable to change the situation. Years passed and he gave up all hope of ever seeing his son again. He thought many times that he might be dead.

Tim was a brilliant young man and excelled in a private school that Kevin had chosen for him. The teacher marveled at his abilities in all areas. He had a quick smile and a great sense of humor. What the teachers did not know was his humor was just a cover up for his sadness. Red hair glistening in the sun, and a smile that covered his entire face, was what Kevin remembered about his son. Each night he would lie in bed and pray for his son's return.

Kevin and Karen grew up together. They were invited to same reunion. Like Karen, Kevin was undecided about going. He would change his mind many times before starting the journey homeward. When the day arrived, he drove several miles, then changed his mind and returned home. After another mind change he got back on the highway. This time there was no turning back.

Karen had already reached the airport, with her ticket in hand. She stood recalling the many wonderful things about her hometown, and began looking forward to seeing old friends. She stood watching couples helping each other wondering what it would be like to have a partner to help her. Karen's entire business trips etc., had been traveled alone. She was okay with doing things on her own, but sometimes she thought it would be appreciated to have a real partner. She prayed one day, and asked God to send someone that would be a loving faithful mate. She soon forgot about it and just carried on with her life as usual. Life did not have much meaning after her son died. Kevin felt the same way when his son left. He did what he had to do, and shut down all emotions the same as his childhood friend so many miles away.

The reunion was wonderful. Karen sat watching the folks from the past. They looked so happy. She wondered if they were as pleased with their lot in life as it appeared or were they play-acting as she had learned to do so brilliantly. She greeted everyone with a smile, and played the role of confidence. As the time went by she found that she was having fun. It was great to be back home with old familiar faces.

Kevin arrived with his parents and Karen quickly greeted them saying how happy she was to see them again. It had been such a long time, but they were now complete strangers. Karen quickly returned to her table. The July afternoon passed quickly and before she knew it people were beginning to depart. Kevin approached her and after a quiet moment of chit chat she stared at him and it was like looking into a mirror. She saw his sadness and it matched her own. He asked for her address saying he would like to write to her and catch up on old times. He asked her if she would answer his letter. "Of course, I will respond to your letter." She quickly answered.

Upon the arrival back to Metropolitan airport, the old sadness set in quickly, but she approached with smiles for all who looked her way.

A short letter arrived from Kevin a few days after her arrival home. Karen responded quickly with a fax to his office. This became a ritual. The second letter told of how his son went away and the sadness that he felt. Karen responded with the news of her losses over the past several years. The letter was filled with details of her past, but showed very little emotion. Facts were given to fill in the gaps of the missing years. When Karen read the letter about Tim she immediately began praying for his return to his father. She knew he would not be happy until his son returned. Tim's grandparents also shared the pain and loss. Kevin's mother feared that she might die, and never see her grandson again, as her health was failing.

Kevin and Karen had decided to meet in their hometown, on Thanksgiving, at his parent's home to get reacquainted. They had become very close through their letters and had confided in each other in a way that neither had done with anyone before.

Thanksgiving was a joyful time for both. They never stopped talking. Words came flooding out. They told one another secrets that neither one had shared with anyone before. The trust was immediate for both. The honesty was something that Karen had never found in anyone. Two people, completely honest, and both needing someone to care for, gave meaning and hope.

After the trip and their arrival home, they found themselves writing more often. The phone calls became more frequent. When Christmas approached it was becoming a sad time for both. One evening, after Christmas, while talking on the phone, they promised each other that they would never be apart on Christmas again. They lived so far from each other and there were many obstacles to overcome, but they felt that if it were meant to be, it would happen. They did not know how or when, but they trusted it would be a reality soon. The couple prayed and asked God to make it happen if it was his will.

Spring was soon to arrive and they decided to spend Easter together and enjoy every moment that they could together. With this visit they became aware of the many things they had in common. Feeling that their love for one another was strong enough, they began planing their future together.

One by one the obstacles were removed, but there was still one sad thing. Kevin's son Tim, was no where to be found. The couple were hoping for a summer wedding. With great urgency Karen began to plead with God to send Tim back into his father's life so he would appear at their wedding.

The time of planing began in early spring. Everything was coming together neatly.

One evening, when Kevin called, she noticed that he was in an exceptionally happy mood. He chatted for a few minutes, and then he said, "I have wonderful news, guess who called me? My son Tim." Karen got shivers through her entire body. Fighting back the tears she said, "My prayers have been answered, I have prayed for this every night." Kevin proceeded to say he was meeting with him on the weekend. With that, Karen was beside herself with joy.

Sunday afternoon was filled with wonder as to how the meeting was going. Karen sat nervously, moving from one place to another, knowing that Kevin and his son were together at that moment, when suddenly the phone rang. She nearly jumped off her chair. Kevin greeted her with, "There is someone here that would like to talk with you." Karen could hardly compose herself when a sweet voice said, "Hello Karen, this is Tim. My father has told me all about you. I am so happy for you. I am so happy also because I have my dad back." After the short conversation Karen hung up the phone and tearfully thanked God for this gift.

The next two months was a time of joy for the pair. It was a time of getting reacquainted with his son. For Karen it was a dream come true. She found Tim to be a treasure. She felt truly blessed with this gift. "God always gives back what is taken away," she thought. As the weeks went by she began to love Tim and Jane, (Tim's girlfriend) in a profound way, and life was good. The next few weeks that followed the foursome shared many happy times together. Kevin and Karen married in the summer as planned. Tim and Jane were in the forefront. The day was perfect.

Settling into married life in the community where they grew up was an exciting time for the Kevin and Karen. Tim and Jane visited from time to time. Kevin's parents were happy having Tim back in their life. They showered Jane with love as though she had always been there.

One evening, in late fall, a call came from Tim, telling his father that he and Jane were engaged to be married. He followed up by asking his father if he could have his wedding in the same little country church where he had been married in the summer. He thought it would be great for his grandparents to see him married. The grandparents, being elderly, it made it impossible for them to travel to his hometown. Tim and Jane had decided on a New Year's Eve wedding and wondered if it could be arranged. Everyone was elated. He followed up by asking his father to be his best man. Jane asked to speak to Karen, and the first thing she said came as a shock. "Will you be my maid of honor?" Karen could hardly contain herself. The excitement grew and her heart began pounding in her chest. She could barely breathe. The plans were in full swing before the conversation ended.

As Christmas closes in on Kevin and Karen their decorations are in place. Tim and Jane are on their way home. Karen is busy baking. The wedding decorations are completed. Kevin is wrapping presents. Many friends and relatives are eager for this, another joyful occasion. Grandmother has a new outfit and grandfather has his best suit pressed. Kevin and Karen are awaiting Tim and Jane's arrival. They will be home soon.

P.S. Happy New Year everyone. Oh yes, it is now midnight New Year's Eve and Tim and Jane are husband and wife.

A Dying Prayer

By Dolores Allen

Wendy stood under the dimly lit street lamp trying to insert the needle without the necessary equipment. The pain was horrible as she desperately searched for a vein. Having nothing to tie tightly around her arm it was difficult to complete the task. Her veins were beginning to collapse, thus making it almost impossible. She began to feel ill. Her hands were trembling. She thought that she was going to have a seizure. Suddenly the weeping began. "Must have the stuff now," she screamed. What used to be so fulfilling was now becoming a nightmare.

"Randy was the reason the changes had occurred," she thought. He was the kind man who introduced her to crack, and she loved him for giving her something that gave her such high self-esteem. This drug promised hope. It was like magic. "Randy and crack became her savior," she once told a friend. Her highs were wonderful at first, and she felt like a princess. It was not long before she began having severe bouts of depression. The more crack she injected, the shorter the highs. Soon the joy and elation, she once felt, became a horror.

The man she once loved so deeply had, all to soon, moved to another love. He kept busy working his same old routine and waving his magic wand. His pattern was always the same. He would gain their trust, and then he would introduce them to the drug. It would not be long before they were hooked. That was how he increased his territory. Every young girl was his toy. Once they were dependent on the crack, he found a new inductee.

By mid summer, the second year of Wendy's addiction, she became overwrought. It took more and more drugs to get the high that she needed. She approached Randy and begged him to allow her to sell the drug. She told him that she needed extra money to support the habit. The response was just a chuckle. She went on to explain to him that she had tried stealing, but that could not accomplish the task anymore. The storeowners in the slum knew her by now, as she had already been caught several times. "You could always move to another location," he told her. "But how will I find another source?" She begged. Randy had the solution of course. Being the sweet kind hearted savior that he was, he introduced her to prostitution.

Morning was breaking and Wendy had slept a restless night under the steps of an old boarding house that gave refuge to the homeless. She was not allowed inside due to a nasty dispute. A middle-aged woman called her a tramp. In a rage she picked up a bread knife and cut a piece of a woman's finger off. It seemed as though Wendy was burning all her bridges behind her. Even the users and hookers had no compassion for her.

Lying there, wondering how she got there, was something she had not allowed herself to think about until now. She leaned back with closed eyes. Something sharp was sticking into her side. Straining to open her eyes, she looked down and saw a broken mirror. Slowly she pulled it up and held it in front of her face. All she felt was shock. The image staring back at her was that of a stranger. The eyes were sunken and black underneath. A face that once held such sweetness and emitted a radiant smile that everyone loved was now sallow and filled with deep creases around the nose and eyes. Her forehead was furrowed. The lips were cracked and bleeding. This could not be the Wendy she knew so long ago. How long had it been since she had become this stranger.

"It's your fault, Randy," she whimpered. A feeling of hatred engulfed her entire being. She despised the man that she had once loved. Staring long and hard at the reflection she knew she must make some hard choices. Her health was failing. She appeared to be twenty years older than her actual age. It had been months since she had even dared to glance at her reflection in a store window. Now, she was staring in this broken mirror and all her fears were confirmed.

"I must get cleaned up and make myself presentable if I intend to do any tricks," she told herself out loud. With that all the energy left her and she sank back leaning against the old broken step. This had become her refuge for the last several weeks. She picked up a wet newspaper that was half hidden by garbage and glanced at the front page. There she saw a picture of a man who looked familiar. Yes, it was a face she knew very well. It was a picture of her father lying on the road beside a crumpled up old car. The headlines read, "my only wish is to see my daughter again." She continued to read. "I think she is dead, but somehow I hope I am wrong," her father was quoted as saying to the attendants. The story continued by saying that a lady stood praying and asking God to save this man and to please return his daughter to him. "He needs this gift, so please "God" return his child. He must be granted his dying wish." As Wendy continued reading she noticed a toll free number in large print at the end of the story asking anyone who might know anything about his daughter or her whereabouts to call.

The disheveled girl struggled to her feet and found a pay phone nearby. She dialed the number and was told that she could go and get a ticket. The voice on the other end of the phone was so kind. He told her that the ticket would be paid for, so just go to the bus station right away as there would be one leaving in a short time. She followed instructions and immediately boarded a waiting bus. She was so eager to see her father that she forgot her craving for awhile.

The bus ride was long and Wendy rarely thought about anything but her dying father. She was shaky and frightened. She began to pray and ask God to help her get to her father before he died. She had so many regrets and wanted to have an opportunity to make it up to him. He had been such a good parent. Struggling for many years to raise Wendy on his own after his wife Jane left. There was no doubt that life had shortchanged him. But now his daughter had only one thing on her mind, and that was to make it up to him. "I hope it is not too late," she whispered to herself.

The steps leading to the front entrance of the massive hospital was all Wendy could manage. She was panting like an athlete after running a marathon. All the years of drug addiction had left her nearly helpless. She wondered if he would recognize her. Upon approaching the information desk an elderly woman came rushing toward her and with a smile she asked, "are you Wendy?" With a nod the two began exchanging pleasantries. The woman told Wendy that her father was badly injured and his case was critical. With that she ushered the girl to a sofa in the corner of the entrance. She began again. "It is not clear at this time if he could come through any operations that he might need in order for him to survive. It is a day by day situation at this time. It could change but they are not optimistic as his injuries are life threatening. One thing they know for sure and that is, he has lost sight in both eyes. Even surgery would not restore any of his vision. Are you ready to come with me now and see your father?" She asked. Fear rose in Wendy's chest and she could barely breath. She followed the woman down the corridor and into the room where her father lay motionless on the sterile white sheets. The frightened girl quietly tip toed over to her father's bedside. She put her hand on his and gently placed a kiss on his cheek. "Father this is Wendy. I am home and you are not going to die." Tears began to stream down the old man's face. "Wendy, you are as beautiful as ever. Thank you for coming. God did answer my prayers. I have been so worried about you for so long." At that moment, Wendy was thankful that her father could not see how she actually looked. He would not have believed it was his beautiful daughter. "Father let me explain why I have not returned sooner. I am so ashamed," she sobbed. Her father quickly interrupted her by saying that there was no time for that and there was no blame only joy at seeing her again. He continued on saying, "thank you for coming to me. Wendy will you promise me one thing?" Wendy began to weep even louder as she felt the unconditional love from her father. "I will do whatever you say from now on. I wish that I had listened earlier," she cried. He began in an earnest tone and when he spoke his words came out slowly, and with such depth that Wendy knew that something wonderful was about to happen. He began by saying, "daughter, please kneel beside my bed and pray with me, and ask God for his forgiveness for you and for me. Let us both make a promise to live a life of giving. Let us promise to pay back for all of our mistakes and begin a new life of living for him. God loves us and I know he will forgive us for any transgressions in the past." Wendy began in a choked voice begging for forgiveness. She promised that she would not go back to the old life. At that moment a woman entered the room. Wendy did not know who it was, but she could see a tall slim lady wearing a black dress lean over her father's bed. The woman began to whisper in her father's ear, "John, this is Jane, can you ever forgive me?" "Of course I can" was the reply and with that he continued on speaking with his daughter. "Wendy, this is your mother."

In no time, the healing had begun and everything was forgiven. The future was planned. There was a new family beginning. That afternoon the three talked and made plans for their life ahead. They made many promises to one another and Wendy felt great.

Early the next morning, as the sun shone brightly in Wendy's room at her father's home, the phone rang. A nurse introduced herself and requested that Wendy and her mother return to the hospital at once as John wished to see them. She hurried into the same dirty clothes he had worn the day before, and rushed out the door with her mother. When they entered the room there was a white shadow hovering over John's hospital bed. John was reaching up to touch the shadow, but it seemed to elude him. "What is it father?" cried Wendy. "What is going on? What is that shadow? Please father don't leave us now," she screamed. Jane took her daughter in her arms and held her for the first time since she was a baby. Wendy was beside herself with anguish. Jane comforted and soothed her with whispering words. She promised her that she would be her very best friend. "I know it is too late to be a mother to you, but I will try to be there for you from now on if you will let me." Wendy held on to her mother and whispered. "Yes, I want that too."

When the funeral was over and the business was settled Wendy went immediately to her father's church and asked the pastor to help her. She needed the prayers of everyone to get her through her recovery program. "With the rehab center and the help of "God," we will make it through," the pastor promised. On her very first visit, Wendy put her faith in God and became a devout follower of the Christian faith. Jane began attending the meetings at the rehab center with Wendy, and she also went to all the church services with her daughter. Together they found a peace and contentment that they had never had before.

When Wendy had been drug free for two years, she returned to school. Upon completion, she began working as a counselor at the recovery home that had helped her. Her mother is now an elder in the church and teaches Sunday school, plus holds down a full-time job in a day care center. Mother and daughter are living in John's home, "one day at a time." They are making up for all the lost years. For this family, it is truly a new beginning.

Homeward Bound

By Dolores Allen

Abbey's mind goes back to the smell of home baked bread. She gazes out over the field of tall trees, her thoughts go adrift. Branches standing naked reaching up to the heavens with outstretched arms as if to say, "I'm coming home." She feels like a branch hanging alone in a sea of unknown faces. No where to go, no where to hide, not belonging anywhere, feeling that there is no new season for her. Spring will bring beauty and color, when the new growth arrives, but not for her. She is unwilling to stretch her lifeless limbs to the sun. For her, spring will not bring new color. Going home should be peaceful.

Abbey longs to find that little girl within. She has tried desperately, but the child has vanished. Crying out, looking to the heavens. "Where did she go?"

Remembering the creaky floorboards in her grandmother's dining room gave Abbey a feeling of distaste. Now, it would be harmony to hear those sounds one more time. She had dreams that her home would be perfect and beautiful, not one with weird sounds, when the wind blew. Slanted floors and smoke from the old wood stove was a real turnoff. Yes, her house was going to be filled with charming antiques and fine crystal.

When Abbey was young, spring was a time of yard cleanup. The job was loathed. So many chores to do, and no time to play. Now she would give anything to go back to that time. If only to see another springtime, in

Spellbinding Stories

the old house.

Longing for the weird sounds, that came on windy days, and yards to be raked, spelled home. Alas, another home was waiting.

Watching the seductive wind pulling and pushing the branches of the tall trees toward the sky, the sad girl begs to be taken along for the ride. "Are you ready?" whispers the breeze.

With eyes closed, suddenly she is back home with the aroma of apple pie awakening her taste buds. When she opens her eyes there is beauty everywhere. The trees have come into full bloom. The sky is blue with fluffy pink cotton candy clouds rolling down the midway. The sound of the creaky floors, and the once hated smell from the wood fire, is bliss. She can see the goodies coming out of the oven. "Someone must have cleaned the yard. How did I get here? How much time has passed?" Was her question. The home baked bread and cinnamon smells steaming out of the apple pie makes her mouth water. I knew I would be going home, but this is not what I expected." Looking out toward the hen house, grandmother is approaching singing a hymn that is familiar. The once disliked litany was now sounding like a heavenly choir. "I can't remember grandmother singing like that. Could this be heaven on earth? Perhaps it is all a dream." She whimpers. Getting a glimpse of herself in the mirror is the reflection of a little girl. She has finally found the child within. "Must savor the time I have here with my memories and appreciate all the things I once took for granted." She whispers. Wandering into the dining room, only to find the same old squeaky floorboards that had never been repaired and hearing the same creaky noises. The same old scents are there, but best of all is the fragrance from her grandmother's talcum powder. "She still uses the same powder." Abbey gasps. "This cannot be happening. I know my grandmother died many years ago, but I see her now." Abbey begins running down the path to greet her grandmother with outstretched arms. Crying ever so softly while passing through the shadow, the child now knows that it is just her imagination. The fantasy is a prelude, to the last journey. The new and lasting journey was about to begin. Grandmother was waiting. This was not heaven on earth, but a preview of the joy that awaited her.

Nature has it's way of bringing every living thing full circle. When the new season arrives it brings new beauty and promise. When the old season ends it leaves a road map of memories, and some broken dreams, but the good part is the appreciation for the simple things. Abbey no longer feels naked and alone like the tall bare branches weaving back and forth toward a gray sky. She is on her way upward to the pink fluffy midway. The barren season is over. She has found the sun.

Hidden Treasures

By Dolores Allen

I often wonder why wonderful friends and family become hidden in our minds. Many times they are not found for several years and then we realize what we have missed. Is it because they are forgotten, or do we just become neglectful? It is almost as if they never were.

My mother had many wonderful friends and family members that she talked about. She would relate story after story of her childhood and the events that took place. I wondered why I was not given the pleasure of knowing them. Many we rarely saw and the majority went by the wayside. I have always felt that we should know our ancestors and old friends. It gives us a sense of who we are, but not only that, it adds value to our life. Some say it is a way of enriching our soul.

When my mother became very ill, it was then that she began to reminisce constantly of the old days. I would write everything in my diary that she told me. She would go on and on about how special these old friends and family members were. Her illness confirmed it to be true. The get well cards and letters came daily. Many were from people that I had never heard about.

We had moved many miles away when I was young. When my mother needed extra support when her journey was nearly over, relatives would come one by one, at great expense to help her through her time of suffering.

As the mail arrived each day, I began to notice that there was a card every week from the same couple that lived in our village. It contained words of encouragement, and they always said that they were praying for her. It got to a point where I was looking forward to the cards as much as she was. I said to my mom one day, "she is like a ray of sunshine." I began asking questions about this couple. She told me many stories of heroic importance. She said that the husband had joined the army when their children were very young. Soon after he was sent overseas. She was a good friend of my mother when they were in school, but somehow they had lost touch over the years. She also said that this lady and her husband were both very spiritual people. One of her fond memories of him was his elegant dress code. He was a tall good-looking gentleman with a stern look, but a heart of gold. She, on the other hand, was a petite woman. I do remember over the years my mother saying how she wished that she was tiny like her friend. My mother was thin, but always wanted to be shorter. The more we talked about them the more interested I became in their story. She said that when her friend's husband came back home after the war his son did not know him. I found that heartbreaking. When my mother passed away their daughter recorded a song for the funeral. I began to talk with her about her parents. She told me that her mother stood on a chair and kissed her father good bye when he went to war. I could just visualize this tiny person beside this tall straight soldier. Later I saw pictures and they were exactly as I had imagined. I did know this family when I was a child, but time and distance had a way of erasing them for my mind. When I began talking with them, I realized that I remembered a few things. Several years later I began writing to their son. He told me many wonderful things about his parents. It was obvious they were special people.

When my mother passed away, I phoned her immediately. She was so sweet and gave me her condolences, showing great sadness.

It was several years later that I had the opportunity to really get to know the aging couple. They welcomed me into their home as if I belonged there. " It was home."

She reminded me of a delicate flower in an English garden. He is the gatekeeper of her heart. I still see him as that tall, straight, handsome man in uniform like his pictures of long ago.

She is ill herself now, but smiles most of the time. When the pain is unbearable, she stills manages a warm greeting to all that come her way. I have chosen to love them. I not only have their love, but that of their son. They taught him well.

They are loving parents, and grandparents and a blessing to many.

This precious flower is no longer a hidden treasure, but a beautiful Daisy and a mother-in-law that I cherish. Reginald, the keeper of her tender spirit is doing his job well. "I write this with love."

Save the Best for Last
Part 2

By Dolores Allen

Sitting here in my Arizona room in Green Valley, far away from the hilltop that I wrote about earlier, has given me time to reflect once again. Perhaps when this story is complete, and I have filled in many of the blanks, it may put the past to rest. This tells the story of how, with the help of God, our dreams can become a reality. The hill was a time of reliving so many sad memories. Today again I have been thinking of all the things that led up to that tragedy on December 13, 1946. As I said before, it was on Friday the 13th that the accident happened. It has taken many years to heal. I wish I could say that it was completely over, but I still have the same nightmare seeing my father on fire. I accept it as something that will stay with me always. The writing has been a source of help. Many wonderful events have taken place since the hill. But first, I must tell you more about my mother, and, of course, more details about my father.

Going back to the night before the fire. The wick was turned down and the flame began flickering in the lamp. Dad thought that perhaps the kerosene that he had purchased at the country store might have had some gasoline mixed with it because it had a different odor. My brother and I knew it was time to go up to the loft and bundle up in the many quilts that lay on the straw tick. Our parents sewed heavy cotton together like a huge pocket. It was filled with straw from a nearby farmer's barn, which made our mattress. When first filled, it was quite comfortable, but after a few nights of my brother and I jumping up and down, the once soft cushion became hard. Life was good even thought, material things were nearly non-existent.

My father was superstitious about Friday 13th, and on the eve of the tragedy he warned us that tomorrow was an unlucky day. He told us to be extra careful writing our Christmas exams.

It was before daybreak that we heard the loud bang. The explosion rocked the house and took our father from us. I have given all the details in part one. It was very difficult to write so I won't repeat again. I do want to say that my mother showed great courage. She carried buckets of water in her bare feet from a nearby well, and put out the fire. Her hands were blistered from the burns she received when opening the door. I believe that she was a hero.

At the risk of being redundant, I must tell you that my father was a hardworking man admired by many. My mother said that she knew when she was 13 years old, James would be her husband. She wrote in her schoolbook Mrs. James Smith.

Father was born out of wedlock. That was the term they used back then. He was ridiculed constantly when he was young. One day several boys placed his head on a cedar fence rail and, laid another rail on his neck then they sat on the top rail. My father said that he thought his neck was broken. After this event he decided he must become physically strong. He worked out faithfully with a determination that no one would ever do anything like that to him again.

John was thirteen months my senior. He was a generous brother. We became inseparable. He thought that he had to take care of me after our father died. I believed that I was the stronger one, but that was never revealed to him, of course.

Sitting that day at grandmother's house, waiting to hear news of our father's condition gave me plenty of time to think about the country store. "Could this place, that had so many good feelings, be responsible for what our father was going through now?" I kept asking myself this question over and over.

It gave some comfort just remembering the nickel cone ice cream on Saturday night. It was the only day that they had the freezer running. My mouth watered just thinking of the soft creamy strawberry flavor as it melted and trickled down my throat. "Must make it last longer," I would think to myself. "Let the cone fill up at the bottom, that's when it tastes the best." I always tried to save the best for last.

The store was a meeting place for people in the surrounding area to gather. Saturday night the folks would dress up in their finest clothes like they were going to a party, and walk to the store. This was the time that they caught up on all the gossip, and told stories.

In the summer, when it was hot and humid, the store was also a meeting place for flies. They gathered in abundance. Sticky streamers called flycatchers were hung from the ceiling. No matter how you tried to avoid them, one always managed to get stuck on your forehead or in your hair.

The long narrow counter provided space for a weigh scale. Next to it was a huge round block of cheese. The outside was covered with a waxed cloth to keep it from becoming hard and dry. On the top lay a thick brown paper. The customers would show the storekeeper what size wedge that they wanted. It was then weighed and wrapped in shiny paper. The roll of paper was held in a large wood spool with a sharp steel cutter on the side. The oversized round roll of string hung from a holder above the counter. It dangled in mid air. The clerk would pull it down when needed, and then push it aside when he finished. The string was white with a wax coating. On the other end of the counter sat several glass jars holding penny candies and dry goods such as rice and beans. Beside the jars, cigarettes were placed in a glass cabinet with a door. Behind the counter tobacco, cigarette papers and cigars were lined up ever so neatly. On the higher shelves, a long pole with a hook at the end, was used to pull down boxes that were unreachable. The floors were hardwood tongue and groove. Once a week, they oiled them. They said it was to keep the dust down. The odor was strong and offensive when they were first treated. In the corner, sat a large barrel with liquid. I think it contained pickles, but I am not sure. It had a sour smell and was dark in color. In the rear of the store, bolts of cloth were stacked high on a shelf. When Christmas was approaching, the storekeeper lined the shelves with hand towels, fancy tea towels, dainty handkerchiefs tied with pretty ribbon and lace, and nice smelling soaps presented in gift boxes. There were always a few dolls, building blocks, toy cars, trucks and games placed randomly on the shelves. One year, he had a train set that ran on batteries. I never did find out who the lucky boy or girl was that got that gem. Behind the shelves, a platform was built, and beside it hung two pairs of boxing gloves. My father was the first to put them on, and the last to take them off.

The store became a haven for storytellers. One trying to outdo the other. The more the narrators repeated them the more they embellished, therefore they became funnier with each rerun. John and I would sit listening. We would try to laugh at the right time. Many, we did not understand. One man, who was considered the town drunk, would weave back and forth with foam running down the side of his chin chanting, "tell us another." He was as funny as the stories. This was the only entertainment they had. I listened intently thinking that one day perhaps I could tell the same funny stories. Somehow they never seemed to come out the same.

One evening, when I began to wander, I noticed a large brown box with several pair of shoes behind the counter. Sitting on the top was a pair of shinny black shoes. They had a strap that went over the top. The excitement in my throat rose. My voice turned into a scream. "Daddy! Come here and see these beautiful shiny shoes! Can I have them, please?" My father looked down at the shoes and said, "they are old fashioned. They will be far too small for you. Look at the narrow toes, they will never fit." "But daddy they will. Please buy them for me?" I began to wail and beg. "Please daddy, they are only 50 cents." We pushed and shoved ... finally they were on my feet. I walked home that night wearing my new black shiny shoes. I don't know what happened, but they were never on my feet again. "I think they must have shrunk, dad," I said in a sorrowful voice. His response was, "Don't worry dear, they were only 50 cents."

Waiting that afternoon, at gram's, for word of his condition, brought to mind another tender moment. I remember, in particular, the day that he announced that he was selling our car. It was an old model "T" with a square top. The most dreadful sounds came from the engine. We loved it! On Sunday afternoons, daddy would take us for a drive on the country roads. My brother and I were given turns, sitting on his lap, steering. Of course, we thought that we were driving, thus, there became a love affair between the hunk of noisy metal, and yours truly. My mother said, "one thing is for sure, your father could never sneak up on us because, we could hear him from miles away." I remember him, standing in the doorway, that morning before he left for town. I was sobbing uncontrollably. He began, in such a serious tone, trying to explain why the car must be sold before winter. He said, " I have no place to store the car. It cannot be driven when the snow comes because the roads are never plowed." All I thought about was that our car was going away and never coming back. I wailed and carried on for a time. When I looked up into my father's face I saw for the first time, tears running down his cheeks.

When he headed down the road that morning it was dreadful hearing the clanging of the engine. The thought that this would be the last time left me feeling empty. My brother and I played all day, but all we could think about was dad coming home without the car. Mother was in the kitchen preparing supper when we heard the most wonderful sound. The excitement was building. "Mommy! Mommy! Daddy didn't sell our car. Can you hear him coming?" My father drove in the driveway with the biggest smile. "I guess no one wanted it as much as we did." He chuckled. It was a night to celebrate. Our car sat in the yard all winter. We spent many hours sitting in the front seat pretending that we were driving.

Suddenly, a sharp knock on grandmother's door, that cold December afternoon, jarred me back to reality. The news that my father gave up the battle and was out of his suffering was supposed to make my brother and I feel good, but somehow it eluded us. We felt a pain that has remained for many years. I told you earlier that my brother ended his sadness by taking his own life. My mother remained a tower of strength.

The old county store, that sold my father the questionable fuel, has since burned. No one knows for sure if there was gas mixed with the kerosene. It was sheer speculation. There is no blame, just a lingering sadness.

Mother endured the loss of my father and her son, but kept right on going as though nothing happened. She worked hard and many times she had two jobs. A gentleman friend nicknamed her "Trooper." She was that and more. Her courage was outstanding. She had a saying. "Hard work never killed anyone."

Many years later, when I was visiting her, she quietly told me that she noticed a bit of blood. That was not the case. She was having a great deal of bleeding. I soon found out that she was a very sick woman. We immediately sold her house and she came to live with me. It took only one week when we learned that she had cancer. She opted for surgery immediately. The doctors reassured me that the operation took care of it, and that she would have a full recovery. I was still very concerned. My son, knowing my fears, went back to the surgeons, and told them that I was not convinced that all was well. They reiterated that the operation had taken away the cancer except for a few cells around the aorta. She began the radiation treatments shortly after the Christmas holidays. They said that this would kill any remaining cells. She had a difficult time. I found myself being confined to home a great deal. My job was badly neglected. Many clients had to be referred to other people. Losing many connections was a concern, but my mother was foremost on my mind at that time. We were never extremely close, but I had a deep admiration for her courage.

When the monthly scans and x-rays were over and everything was clear it was always a relief.

One Friday afternoon, the nurse called and said to bring my mother back on Monday. They had to redo some x-rays. We entered the cancer clinic early on the Monday morning. I questioned the nurse asking, "why does my mother have to have these x-rays over again?" She said, "oh, the x-rays did not turn out, that's all." I felt relieved. Radiology was on the second floor so we proceeded up the stairs. She was ushered into the change room. For four hours they scanned and x-rayed and put her thought a terrible ordeal. Fear was like a heavy fist pounding my chest. It was well founded. In less than a week, we learned that the cancer had spread. There was nothing they could do for her, except keep her comfortable with morphine.

One morning, when a nurse visited our home, she told me, "you must allow your mother to die. You have to give her permission. She is being stimulated far too much. If you keep this up, she will never let go. She has a fear that you will not be able to deal with it. She will continue her struggle to live." Mother had wasted away to approximately 60 pounds.

After the nurse left, I laid in bed beside my mother and we talked. We had become very close during this time. She told me only days earlier, that I was the best daughter a mother could have. If there was ever any misunderstandings in the past, this took care of everything. The love for my mother was different than what I felt for my father, but it was just as intense.

Lying beside her, touching her sharp bones made me weep. I whispered in her ear ever so softly, "mom, daddy is waiting for you and so is John. Feel free to join them, I know that is what you want. Please do not worry about me, everything will be okay. I will miss you, but remember that we will all be joined together one day." We said a prayer. She nestled in and began to relax.

The phone rang. I jumped out of bed to answer. "Who was it?" she asked. "It was your brother. He is flying into Detroit tonight. He will be here this evening. Forget everything I told you, mom. You must wait." She rallied and spent almost two weeks with a brother she loved. After he left to go home, we went through the same ritual again. She made another effort to go, on Monday afternoon after everyone had left. I began to cry. "Oh mom, wait a little longer?" She squeezed my hand. We spent most of the day in bed together talking. Her responses were faint. That same evening, as the family gathered around her bedside, she raised her hands toward the ceiling and with eyes wide open, she joined my father and brother. It was a peaceful exit. The doctor came to the house and told us that we did not need to have her taken to the funeral home immediately. We kept her with us until eleven o'clock that night. It gave everyone time to lay down beside her and have their last moments with her. It was a peaceful and joyful time seeing my mom out of her suffering and the knowledge that she was with my father again. I said before that my son joined her when he was 37 years of age. He suffered from cancer also, but for a much shorter time. Mom was ill for two years, but my son suffered only 6 weeks. I know that she was on hand to welcome him at his time of passing.

Sitting here in this bright Arizona sunshine reliving the pain of the past does not seem quite so horrid as it did on the hilltop.

I must move ahead though, and tell you how I happened to be here. I ended my first story telling you about the stranger I met on the hill, and the strong connection that gave me a feeling of hope. Many wonderful things have happened since then.

Today I will try to put away all the sad times and from this day forward concentrate on only the happy times.

Our letters began flying back and forth in a flurry. Phone calls became quite frequent and then they began daily. When we had connected in such a wonderful way via phone and mail we decided to meet back in our little village. It was a joyous time. We giggled like we were school kids again. When we left to go our separate ways there was feeling of sadness. We knew the friendship would grow and continue. Trips became more frequent and one day we knew that we wanted to be together. We began to pray and ask "God" if it was meant to be let it happen. We left everything in "His" hands. Our love and respect kept growing with each visit. In two years God helped us overcame all the obstacles, and we were married on my birthday. It was on the 13th, of July, but not on a Friday. As I said before, I prayed that God would send me a partner that would be faithful and loving. He gave me that. In addition, He gave me two wonderful stepsons and their families. My dream of becoming a writer may also come true. I am sitting here writing and looking out over the garden. Watching the quail scurrying across the patio, in sunny Arizona, I keep asking myself, "can this be real? It is real. We have "saved the best for last."

About the Author

Dolores Allen … The Author was born in eastern Canada. Her childhood ended at age of 9 ½, when her father died in a house fire. She has learned much from her own life altering experiences. She writes about real people. Dolores gives credit for her talent of storytelling to her father.

She lived most of her adult life in Windsor, Ontario.

After being a Real Estate Broker for 26 years, she attended the University of Windsor, studying writing.

She has published stories in a weekly newspaper and is currently writing for a local paper in the Maritimes.

She incorporates personal tragedies into many of her fiction stories.

Life experiences and losses have given a vast vessel for story telling. Her words are inspiring and emit courage.

The variety of stories hold your interest. She has a creative imagination.

In the year 2000 she attended a school reunion back east, which was the beginning of a wonderful loving relationship with George.

They were married in 2002 and now reside in Green Valley, Arizona for the winter months.

She writes with emotion and once a story is started, you are hooked. I promise that you will not want it to end. She is a talented storyteller.

Printed in the United States
18735LVS00005B/88-222